For Queen and Country

Book 2: A Necessary End

By Ellora Lawhorn

Paperback ISBN 978-1-80424-702-0
ePub ISBN 978-1-80424-703-7
PDF ISBN 978-1-80424-704-4

Published by Orange Pip Books
An imprint of MX Publishing
335 Princess Park Manor, Royal Drive,
London, N11 3GX
www.mxpublishing.com

Cover design by Awan

For Mom, who made sure the first things I held were books, pens, and cats. I love you more than comprehension.

'Cowards die many times before their deaths;
The valiant never taste of death but once.
Of all the wonders that I yet have heard
It seems to me most strange that men should fear;
Seeing that death, a necessary end,
Will come when it will come.'
      – William Shakespeare, from Julius Caesar

Music for Readers of *A Necessary End*

The Merriment of Murder by Gothic Storm
Three Days to Cross by Austin Wintory
Lament for the Woods by Atli Örvarsson
The Green Dress by Ramin Djawadi
Lament of the Ice Giants by David Arkenstone
Caves by CLANN
Calon Lan (feat. Tia Kalmaru) by Gareth Lumb
Storm Drums by Medwyn Goodall
Let's Solve the Case by Gothic Storm

Individual book playlists and a larger playlist titled *Queen and Country* can be found on Spotify, Apple Music, and Amazon Music. There are some variations on the main playlist based on song availability, but the playlists found in these books will always be available in their entirety on all platforms. Ellora's profiles are also host to several *Q&C* inspired playlists based on book, character, and theme.

A Note to the Reader

As I mentioned before you read *The Devil at Prayers,* Emily's accounts do much to humanise these historical figures by showing that their struggles were much the same as we have today.

Be advised that *A Necessary End* features themes of self-harm, abuse, and graphic descriptions of dead bodies, and take care of yourself accordingly.

Yours,

Renee Watson

Prologue: The End That Crowns Us

It is the end that crowns us, not the fight.
– Robert Herrick

'No. Palm up, like this.' Andrew took my fist and flipped it around. 'See that flip movement? You're going to do that midway through the punch. There's a lot more force if the impact isn't made with your thumb on the inside.'

'Doesn't that slow it down if I switch positions in the air?'

He unwrapped the brace around his shoulder and shook out his arm. 'Sometimes a small break in velocity will hit heavier when you're already close to the target.'

I frowned as he massaged his shoulder. 'Are you sure you're fit to be using that arm?'

'Of course, Doctor Watson said on Monday I could do without the sling.'

'Yes, but he didn't say you could teach a girl to fight quite yet.'

Andrew tied the brace again and shot me a devilish grin. 'No, but I don't see him doing it. Now, try it again. Aim for the side of my throat, I can't guard it.' He took his stance and put his arms up in front of his face.

'No, I'll knock you out!'

Andrew slumped his shoulders. 'You're not knocking *me* out, you'd be knocking out someone trying to hurt you.'

I exhaled steadily. 'Right, got it.'

I threw my first punch to his left side. When he moved both arms to block it, I swung my other fist sideways, just under his jaw on the right side, flipping it upside down before it made contact.

'Perfect,' Andrew smiled. 'Now try some of those kicks.'

I groaned. 'You didn't say we were practising those today!'

'No, I didn't, but you shouldn't rule anything out.'

'Oh, I see, another patented Lynch lesson,' I quipped wryly, reaching for the box of safety pins I'd left on the corner shelf to pin up my skirts.

'Not today,' Andrew warned. 'I let you use pins the first few times, but when a man springs on you in a dark alley, you won't have time to pause and pin up your hems.'

I took a breath and willed my feet not to get tangled in metres of cloth.

Andrew picked up the straw-stuffed sack he'd been using as a shield for me to hit.

Suddenly, a key turned in the lock of the records room.

Andrew froze and put a finger to his lips. I turned in the direction of the door slowly, trying not to let my heels make any noise in the echo-prone room.

We both released a breath when we heard Holmes' chatter and Lestrade's weary sigh. The slightly limping footsteps behind them must have been John.

'Of course he's not active again, don't be ridiculous!' Holmes said with a high laugh. 'But I'm comparing his victims for a monograph. Access to the file is, of course, imperative. Let's see, it should be back here…'

His voice trailed off as he rounded the corner. I heard a stumble from behind as Lestrade almost crashed into him.

He cocked his head to the side assessing the sack Andrew held, the cloth wrapped tightly around his still healing shoulder, and the bruise forming on one of my knuckles from where I'd swung at his jaw, tripped, and hit the edge of a shelf.

'Watson,' Holmes said calmly, 'I do believe Mr Lynch is jeopardising the recovery of his tendons.'

John came around the corner then, with Lestrade peering over his shoulder in confusion.

'What the devil do you think you're doing?' the doctor demanded.

'Really, sir, I'm not being reckless. I have it wrapped, see? And I'm being gentle and stretching it regularly! Besides, I'm not throwing any punches here!'

The good, but irritated, doctor held up a finger, pointing from him to me. 'Not you. *Why* are *you* and Lynch in a secret, hidden corner of the archives room throwing punches? Is he teaching you to fight?'

I shrugged. 'Neither of you had offered.'

'Clearly, we did not think it was necessary.'

'Well, whether you want me getting into trouble, I'm still going to. After the incident at the docks, and… everything that followed, Andrew thought I should know.'

My brother sighed and pinched the bridge of his nose.

'Let's see it,' Holmes interjected, crossing his arms.

'You really trust him to teach her?' John scoffed.

'Watson, he saved her life during the Ivanov raid.'

'And endangered it in the first place!'

'Which is wholly irrelevant now. Let's see what you've been working on for the past six weeks.'

I met Andrew's eyes, silently asking if we should try the first arranged pattern of moves he'd been helping me memorise. He nodded, and we both took up our stances.

We swung and dodged each other's advances. When Andrew moved to attack from the side, I pivoted and let my feet carry me backwards to compensate. I blocked and ducked under his punches, twirled under his arm, aimed a kick at his left kidney.

Lestrade and John were doing their best to look unmoved. Holmes, on the other hand, was truly passive, watching our every move critically. After we finished, he stepped forward.

'Andrew, your form is good, but I have a couple of pointers. Emily, you're still shaky – we'll work on that. When you backstepped, you did it as though you didn't know what was behind you.'

'What if I don't?'

'Your opponent doesn't need to know that. A woman who can fight will surprise him momentarily. But a woman who *knows* she can fight is an entirely different enemy.' He turned to Andrew. 'Stance.'

He obediently put his weight on one foot, raising his fists.

Holmes jabbed at his underarms and the side of his ribcage. 'Your elbows are too high up, this entire area – arguably the most critical – is still wide open. Elbows down, fists up. There you are. Shoulders forward a little, protect your jugular. That's it.' He turned back to me. 'Now, face me.'

'What?'

'Get into position, I want you to face me. I won't hurt you, but I want you to try and hurt me as much as you can.'

6

'Holmes, I couldn't possibly—'

'Emily, this isn't in any way a slight against you, but I seriously doubt I have anything to fear here.'

I sighed and copied Andrew's adjusted stance. 'Now the neck isn't free.'

'No, it is not. Be prepared for an opponent who has boxed before.'

John rolled his eyes and elbowed Holmes aside. 'Or who has been in the military. Boxing's all patterns and clean fights. There are no clean fights on the battlefield.'

I looked him up and down. 'What do you want me to do?'

'Whatever you can. It's time to stop thinking and act.'

'But I should be—'

As I began talking, my brother, doctor and army veteran, pinned me to the wall within a second. He held one arm across my throat, with his other hand pressed a thumb over a pressure point in my shoulder hard enough to show his strength.

'*Should* you be practising your calculation? You can already do that, you're a Watson. Stop second guessing yourself. Someone who wants to inflict harm won't wait for you to be ready. You must be ready for him. Now try to slip out.'

I tried to slide down, but his arm tightened against my neck.

'Wrong. Slide down and you're unconscious; depending on his grip, he could easily break your neck.'

I grabbed for his other hand, to wrench him away. He caught it and completely immobilised me.

'Wrong again. He already has you in a corner. Any move he can see you starting to make will cost you the fight. Maybe your life. What should you do? What should you *always* do when you're fighting against a man?'

Hesitantly, I eased a knee upwards to almost touch him.

He released me. 'Exactly. Now why were you so slow there?'

'Because you're my brother.'

'I'm a doctor and a soldier. I can drop a man to his knees with a thumb on his wrist, choke him unconscious in five seconds, or snap his neck even faster.'

'If I'm to be fighting dirty, then teach me how.'

John chuckled. 'All in time.'

Lestrade was removing the box Holmes was seeking from a shelf in the corner. 'That explains the thumps Sergeant Wilcox heard.' He coughed as dislodged dust floated thick in the air. 'Poor fellow was starting to think we had a ghost.'

Holmes snorted. 'A ghost in the records room? How droll. Come, Watson, I require my Boswell.'

As the trio walked back towards the door, John paused, turning to Andrew. 'Do be careful with that shoulder. Oh, and Lynch? Thank you.'

'Watson! The game is afoot! Or, well, the research!' Holmes called through the stacks.

With a meaningful look at me and a grateful smile to Andrew, my brother turned and jogged to meet his friend.

As we heard the door creak open and shut in the distance, Andrew raised the sack again and braced himself. 'Well, that was something. Right roundhouse.'

I followed his instructions, trying to get the hang of not tripping.

'Good. Again.'

Chapter 1: The Pain of Hell

Ah, to think how thin the veil that lies between the pain of hell and Paradise.
— George William Russell

I could see Ariana on the other side of the glass. She was right there. Yet we couldn't touch, couldn't hear each other's words.

I picked up the chair and smashed the glass. But Ariana disappeared in a pool of blood the shape of the one that had appeared underneath my stepfather. Koval. Andrew.

She was gone. My sister was gone.

I cried out with a pain in my ribs and collapsed.

I awoke with a start. My panic shook me from my dream for another night.

I was in my dark bedroom in Baker Street. The only window in sight looked out onto the silent and still street below.

A crash sounded from somewhere above me, and a moment later, John appeared, eyes wide and night-clothes askew.

'Is everything all right, Emily?'

'It's fine,' I replied, hoping that the tremors in my voice were not audible. 'There was a spider on the bedpost, but I squashed it. Just go back to bed.'

Reluctantly, my brother mumbled and left me alone. For this I was fortunate. I did not want him to see how fragile I was. My hands were shaking uncontrollably, tear streaks running down my face. I could feel the emptiness inside me. The darkness of the room seemed to press against me from all sides, like an ever-circling monster. Shakily, I got up and turned on the gas, providing a dim light that immediately relieved the pressure. The emptiness, however, was still present.

The past month of recovering from my external injuries had done nothing to assuage those I felt internally. I hadn't told anyone. I didn't know what they would say. I had heard of women being condemned to asylums for experiencing such feelings. But I could still function. I could still solve cases. It would appear from the outside that nothing was wrong with me, although things were not as they seemed.

John would understand. The Second Afghan War was long past, but I knew that more often than not, he lived his life as though it were as present as London's fog hanging over our heads.

Knowing this, however, was far easier than speaking of it.

I collapsed onto my bed, no longer able to hold back my sobs. Bouts of tears had been coming far more frequently since the Ivanov case. I held them back when I had someone to protect, someone for whom to be strong. But Ariana was not here. Holmes and John did not need me to be strong for them. There was only me, and I was growing tired of being strong for myself.

10

I pulled the blankets up to my chin and held tightly onto my pillow for the remainder of the night.

The following morning, I could barely eat any of the kippers and eggs that Mrs Hudson had served. I avoided the gazes of my brother and his flatmate, and excused myself as early as I could, retreating to my bedroom.

The emptiness of the night before had not left. In fact, it had only multiplied, was pressing against the insides of my rib cage and flooding through my body, begging to be let out.

Once I was sure that no one would disturb me, I reached underneath my pillow and pulled out the razor I had stolen from John's room two weeks prior.

No, Emily, stop, I told myself.

But I couldn't.

My hands shook and tears streamed down my face. Before I knew it, I had drawn the edge across my skin and drops of blood oozed from beneath.

Just over a fortnight ago, Holmes had slammed a book down on his experiment table in frustration, sending a precariously balanced beaker over the edge. He had then promptly thought of the solution to his case, triggered by some invisible thought process to which I was not privy, and dashed out of the flat. I had been left to sweep up the shards of glass. As I had collected them, one sliced the edge of my hand. I had not thought much of it at the time, but that night, I found myself lying awake, staring at the scabbing-over scratch, unable to stop thinking about the sensation.

It was like a bee sting, many of which I had experienced as a young girl in the countryside around Thorndon Hall. But somehow, it still felt good. I couldn't explain why drawing blood suddenly felt so good. It managed to make the hollow inside me hurt a little less, for a little while. At the same time, it was worse, a painful reminder of what I'd endured and the secrets that I was still keeping.

It was also harder than expected, the pressure required when intention was present.

I sat on my bed numbly for a moment, staring at the drops of blood on my arm, then looked around frantically and noticed that I had nothing to wipe the blood off with. I didn't have any bandages to cover it up so as not to soil my dress.

Before entering the sitting room, I stood still in the hallway for a moment to ascertain whether Holmes and John were still at the breakfast table…

They were.

Holmes was grumbling about the personal columns in the papers, and John was laughing at him softly.

'My dear, I never tire of your cynical wit.' He seemed to have forgotten the word *detective;* he must not have slept well after he came to check on me.

I pushed the door open. 'John, where's your medical bag?'

He looked up sharply. 'Are you hurt, Emily? What is it?'

'Oh, it's nothing. I just tripped in my room and scraped my arm on the corner of my desk. I only need to get a small bandage.'

'Nonsense, let me look at it. It'll need to be cleaned.'

I opened my mouth to object, but he was already pulling out his black bag from under Holmes' chemical table. He beckoned me over and I could do nothing but follow, holding my arm gingerly.

'Hold it out,' he ordered, the familiar firm expression of a physician.

Biting the inside of my cheek, I did as instructed, keeping my sleeve lifted so as not to bleed on my dress. John extracted a small wad of cotton from his bag to dab gently at the drops of blood that glistened on my skin. Then he lifted my arm and inspected the wound.

His brow wrinkled as he peered closer.

My breath caught in my throat. Was it not consistent with a scrape? Did he somehow know what I had done?

But my brother said nothing. He merely disinfected the wound and stuck a small bandage over it.

'Thank you,' I murmured, leaving the room again as fast as I could. Once I was in the hallway, I heard the men's voices and lingered, listening.

'Is everything all right, my fellow?' Holmes asked.

There was a beat of silence before my brother answered. 'Perhaps. It just seems a bit blustery to be wandering about with one's sleeves pulled up.'

Holmes' reply was too quiet for me to hear, and their tones were not audible after that. I closed my eyes, leaning my forehead against the outside of the doorframe, and took a deep breath before returning to my room.

I spent the rest of the morning curled in the wicker chair with my journal and a copy of Wilkie Collins' *The Moonstone,* writing and reading and looking out at the desolate, grey appearance of the world outside. Although there weren't any trees by which to judge the strength of the wind, I could see abandoned newspapers and other pieces of litter blowing fiercely on the street, and I could hear the rattle of the windowpanes as they shook.

Just before the normal time for luncheon, there was a knock at my door.

'Come in,' I called.

John stood at the threshold. His eyes wandered absently to my desk for a moment, but then he fixed his gaze on me. 'Holmes asked me if you would like to come into the sitting room. A letter arrived by post and he'd like to discuss the possibility of a new case.'

I rose from my seat, marking my page and following my brother into the sitting room.

Holmes was sitting in his armchair by the fireplace, leaning forward eagerly, with an unlit pipe in his mouth and a piece of thick stationery in his hand. He looked up as John and I entered.

'There you are, Emily,' he said, voice keen and eyes glinting. 'I have received a letter from North Yorkshire, and the case looks promising, if you should care to hear the particulars.'

I nodded and took a seat on the sofa.

Looking at me out of the corner of his steely eyes from over the top of the letter, Holmes began to read. I leaned forward and rested my chin on my hands to listen, then quickly put my left arm in my lap and relied completely on my right for support when I felt the burning of the fresh wound.

Although my eyes were fixed on Holmes, I could feel John's cautious, steady gaze on me and my injured arm. I tucked it in against my dress so that it could no longer be seen.

Holmes narrated:

'"Mr Holmes,

I have heard of your success in London and I implore you to help my family with the dreadful situation into which we have fallen.

Three days ago, my brother, Simon Camberwell, left to walk into the nearest town. Rosedale Abbey is named after our family's old estate, which lies near the town with one of the moor's forests between. He was to meet a group of his old school friends from Eton for drinks at the public house. The owner of the pub saw them all outside arguing after a few drinks, but that is the only incident of note.

My dear brother has made no enemies and surely the argument was merely the influence of the drinks they had consumed. He never returned home. It wasn't that he spent the night in town, too disoriented to make his way home, or that he was kept in local police custody for disorderly conduct, no. He merely never returned, nor have we seen or heard from any of his friends since that night.

It is quite a peculiar situation as his friends are usually eager to drop by and visit. Edward, the closest of these friends, is much like another brother to me. The local constabulary has no idea what has happened to him, and will not investigate, but I refuse to believe that all hope is lost.

I beg of you to come and show the others that my brother is not lost forever.

Sincerely yours,
Miss Nicole Camberwell. " '

As Holmes finished reading, I pulled back slightly, the name tugging at my memory. Knowing that it wouldn't come to me as long as I tried, I shook off the feeling and concentrated on the case before us.

'So, no evidence?' I asked.

'As far as this letter dictates,' replied Holmes, tossing the letter aside and jumping up from his chair with the energy of a foxhound on the scent. 'I would prefer to have some observations fresh from the scene, but I can't expect a prospective client to know what to look for. I've already had Harry purchase our train tickets. We leave tomorrow morning.'

Harry was one of the Baker Street Irregulars, a group of homeless boys, most of them orphans, employed by Holmes to help on cases. As children, they could watch and listen without anyone even acknowledging their presence.

I had met Harry once before, about a week after I moved into Baker Street. I had been coming down the stairs as he was delivering a note to the detective, and in his enthusiasm he had run straight into me. He was an Irish boy, about nine years of age, with a curly mop of red hair, a bouncy and excitable disposition, and a charming smile that could con the devil.

But this wasn't about Harry. We had the prospect of a case.

I couldn't help but smile.

It wasn't just *they* anymore. It was *we*.

I had not been taken along on another case as of yet, but I'd heard the statements of clients, been told the evidence. Even offered my own theories.

The excitement of cases had done me well, especially after I'd been kidnapped during the Ivanov case. It gave me something to do, things to occupy my mind – and often my hands. Holmes must have known that I needed something more than peripheral involvement, and convinced John that I should not have to stay at the flat with Mrs Hudson.

And, although my veins and skin itched for the blade again, I knew that I could last. A new energy coursed through my body as I stood up and went to pack for the morning's journey.

Chapter 2: Out of Darkness

And out of darkness came the hands that reach thro'
nature, moulding men.
> – Alfred Lord Tennyson

I spent much of the long train ride thinking of Andrew as I sketched the autumnal portrait that existed outside the window of our compartment. That morning, prior to our departure, I had visited him at Scotland Yard to inform him of our leaving. I thought of his eyes, the honesty and concern for me that they beheld. The spark of adventure.

Looking down at the sketchbook in my lap, I saw that I had inadvertently incorporated his eyes into the drawing, looking out from the trees lining a creek bed. Hastily, I flipped the book closed and shoved it into the open bag at my feet before it could be seen, making a mental note to destroy that page later.

We spent most of the journey in silence, which was broken once or twice by a plump woman with a tray who poked her head in to deliver cups of tea to those who wished.

Holmes had his fingers steepled and was staring out the window intently. His gaze and attention never wandered, nor did he ever move.

At the same time John read several issues of the *Lancet*, scribbling notes in the margins with a pencil.

After about two hours I could not help but notice that my legs were cramping horribly from sitting still for so long in a small compartment. There was not enough room for me to politely make my way out into the corridor and walk around a bit, much less stretch out my legs. I merely groaned, made a face, and sat perfectly still, crammed into the corner by the window, even though my limbs protested.

When we finally departed the train, the first thing I noted was that the town was small, smaller than Thorndon had been. Few others trickled off the train along with us. On the street, several boys were chasing each other with sticks, but otherwise the town seemed devoid of human presence.

A kind of dank, foul smell hung in the air, from which I gathered that this must be a mining town. The road looked dusty and bumpy, but I was quite used to such things in Thorndon.

We carried our bags between us to a cab that was standing ready. It didn't look like it was from around here. A permanent dust had settled over everything, but the cab was clean. I assumed, then, that it had been sent from the Camberwell estate. And they, of course, must be the family who owned the mines.

I glanced over to Holmes and saw his gaze roving around the street and coming to rest on the cab, deducing the same.

The cabbie seemed quite puzzled as to why a young lady was travelling with two men, but he didn't question it. He looked us up and down shiftily as if we did not belong.

'You must be Mr Holmes and company.'

And as I looked from our clean and crisp city outfits to his own threadbare, shoddy ensemble to the dusty dirt road beneath us, I had every sense that we were even more out of place than we could ever know.

The ride from the town to the old Camberwell family estate was not long, surprisingly. I had grown used to the constantly bustling atmosphere of the crowded city with the slow, jerky cab rides as drivers manoeuvred the horses through traffic.

Even the sudden jolts underneath us were not unlike the roughly paved streets of London. The ride was bumpy and the ground horribly uneven, as the roads themselves were set along the bulbous hills of the moors that occasionally erupted like boils on the earth.

Through the window, the landscape around us was barely visible in the dim late-afternoon light. The entire sky was a mass of thick, grey clouds.

Indeed, in such grim illumination, the land looked as barren and desolate as the sky above. The scanty grass was brown and withered, blending with the bare patches of earth.

There were occasional clusters of stunted trees, their trunks old and knotted, their branches stretched out and curved like long, bony fingers. They had already lost their leaves for the most part, but those that remained were brown and dead.

Craning my neck to look further up the road, I could see that we were approaching a forest, stretching out before us like the spread of some evil shadow across the land. The trees there were taller, almost as if they had grown to shelter something within. As we approached, a strong breeze rustled the withered leaves. Before I could repress a shudder, the carriage entered the woods and we found ourselves engulfed from all angles, unable to see anything but black shapes and shadows stretching far out into the distance.

It wasn't much longer before the forest ended, and an old stone house unfolded before us. It was large and gothic in design, with crenelated towers rising to touch the swirling clouds.

The cab stopped. John offered me a hand down and I gazed at the towers and edifices, and the effect it had was as sinister as the surrounding moors.

A slim figure cloaked in shadow was leaning against the doorway. As the shabbily clothed cab driver began unloading our luggage from the back, it rushed down the stairs, and across the rolling hills of the lawn, towards us.

As the shadow came closer, I could see that it was a girl.

I gasped softly.

It appeared that she remembered me as well.

Miss Nicole Camberwell. I knew I had heard the name somewhere before. It was during the Ivanov case, at the docks. She had seen Moriarty's man leaving the scene.

But what had a girl like her been doing at the West India Docks?

I stared at her, hoping my question got across. She stared back at me for a moment before shaking her head lightly and turning to Holmes.

'Mr Holmes, I presume?' she extended a hand.

'I am,' he replied, bending to kiss the hand she held out, his face devoid of any emotion.

'And I must conclude that this is Dr Watson.'

John too kissed her delicate hand.

After a moment, Nicole turned back to Holmes, her attention still focused on me.

'I am Nicole Camberwell. I must thank you for coming. Police here are scarce, and those who came from surrounding towns thought nothing of the matter. My father was adamantly against hiring an investigator, but I simply could not let Simon's disappearance pass without consequence.'

Holmes drew back. Although his face remained expressionless, I could sense shock and a bit of disapproval in his demeanour.

'Do you mean to say, Miss Camberwell, that your... family has no idea that you asked me here?'

Nicole opened her mouth, but she was cut off by the arrival of another man. I knew he must be her father.

Mr Camberwell was tall, towering even above Holmes, with a square jaw and a crooked nose that had obviously been broken sometime in his youth. His eyes were dark and beady, and he reminded me of a snake. Not as much as Moriarty, of course, but enough that the association made me shiver. In all respects, the man was imposing. I shrunk back slightly.

'Nicole,' said the man coldly, 'who are these people?'

'Sherlock Holmes.' He quickly stepped in for Nicole, who looked like she wanted nothing more than to melt into the ground.

Mr Camberwell tightened his jaw. 'And what is *Sherlock Holmes* doing on my lawn?'

'I asked them here, Father,' explained Nicole, her voice shaking. 'About Simon —'

He held up a strong hand at his daughter, who flinched. 'Go inside. I will deal with you later.'

I watched Nicole as she turned to walk toward the house, noticing the involuntary trembling in her hands. I knew that it was not from the chill wind that swept across the lawn.

'If I may, sir,' my brother spoke up, 'I am Doctor John Watson, Mr Holmes' friend and chronicler. And this is my sister, Miss Emily. We're here regarding your son's disappearance.'

Mr Camberwell's face darkened to match the sky above. 'And what concern of yours are the private matters of my family?'

I cautiously eyed Holmes, whose face took on an equally stormy quality. The man was extremely controlled regarding his

21

emotions, but having elected to put his genius into detective work rather than diplomacy, the integrity of his cases was a very personal matter to him, and this crossed the line. I could sense John watching him too.

'My good sir,' Holmes began, forcing out the words, 'I would hardly call the disappearance of your son a private matter. It is a possible crime, and allowing it to remain un-investigated is to taint the integrity of justice. I am a private consulting detective – the first to carry such a title. I have fought my way up until this point to carve out a name for myself. This is what I do. My companions and I have travelled here from London simply for the sake of serving justice.

'Such a man as yourself surely must work hard to uphold his social status. If you wish to maintain such a status, it would be shameful of you to turn us away now. Especially if we have a chance of returning your son to you – and let me say, the odds of success are far greater with us than they would be with any constabulary or police force in the country. Consider your situation and act accordingly.'

Mr Camberwell appeared stunned into silence by the force of Holmes' speech. Realising his vulnerability, he squared his shoulders and hardened himself again.

'Four days. I will give you four days in this house to find my son.' He glared at each of us in turn. 'Marshall, see their bags to the door. Curtis will take them from there.'

He turned stiffly and walked back to the house, leaving us to follow in his wake.

Shivering in the cold, I knew that we were not only out of place here, but more than a little unwelcome.

Chapter 3: The Anchor of Our Souls

Hope is the anchor of our souls. I know of no one who is not in need of hope – young or old, strong or weak, rich or poor.

– James E. Faust

By the time we had been shown to our rooms, night was falling on the moors – though there was not much difference with the dark and tumultuous sky.

I watched the shadows creep ever closer and finally engulf the house altogether as I stood at the foot of my bed folding clothes and staring out the old, thick-paned window. The clouds in the distance were likely marking the approach of a storm. My suspicions were confirmed when I heard a faint rumble. There wasn't much that could be done in the way of investigating at night with a storm fast moving in. I yearned for something to occupy my mind as well as my hands. My body was filled with restless energy.

I glanced at the clock on the wall opposite my bed. Dinner, we had been told, would not be served until seven. In an hour.

Letting out a sigh, I tossed a crumpled stocking onto the bed.

Exploring. I wanted— No, I *needed* to explore.

Normally, exploring freely in another family's house would be frowned upon, to say the least, but I had a feeling that as long as I didn't run into Nicole's father, no one would mind.

I was struck by the level of fear the girl had shown towards her father and the loneliness other than visits from her brother's school friends that she had exhibited in her letter. It seemed plain that her mother was dead, or else was ill and not able to interact with others, much as my own mother had been for months prior to her death. She also hadn't mentioned any other siblings in her letter, so I concluded that no one presently resided in the house aside from her, her father, and the housekeeping staff.

It seemed relatively safe for me to take a walk around.

As I reached for the door handle, my pulse leaped in anticipation, causing my left arm to ache again. I sucked in a breath and twitched my fingers until the pain had somewhat subsided. Then I turned the handle and stepped into the silent hallway.

The walls were made of wood, painted over in a crème sort of colour that should have made the whole area seem brighter. The paint colour was an unconvincing attempt at cheeriness, for the gas lamps adorning the walls at intervals down the whole of the corridor cast a dim glow rather than a bright light.

No one was about, but the wind blowing against the windowpanes broke the otherwise disconcerting silence.

I let my feet guide me, thoughts rippling between the soft rustle of my skirts. I stopped every few steps to consider how far

I should go. We were on the second floor of the house, and it was unlikely any bedrooms would be located on the floors above. So, I hesitantly began to climb the staircase at the end of the carpeted hall. The mahogany railing was shiny from so many accumulated polishes; the carpet was worn on the right side, close to the railing.

With the absence of a Mrs Camberwell, and Mr Camberwell having such a seemingly violent temper, it appeared likely that not enough attention was paid to these sorts of things. It also seemed that the house didn't receive enough visitors for it to be a priority.

The walls along the staircase were blank, painted with the same light colour. But there were some patches, rectangular in shape and about two feet in height, that were brighter than the rest of the wall. Something had been hanging there up until very recently. Portraits, most likely; judging from the stark contrast between these patches and the background, ones that had been hanging there for a very long time.

So, what had caused them to be taken down? The death of the family member? No, for very rarely did families hang portraits of living relatives. The custom was to hang them as a sign of respect after the person in question had passed on. A gesture of remembrance, and a sort of symbol that the person was still watching over the family, even in death. A little more than unsettling, in my opinion, but a popular custom, nonetheless.

It was obvious that this floor wasn't used as much. The spacing of the gas lamps was sparser here, none of them lit. This made the hall even more eerily still, set in contrast to the rain pattering heavily against the windows like hundreds of little running feet.

In the darkness, I could barely make out the figure standing at one of the windows about halfway down the corridor. It was short, plainly feminine. Nicole.

'Hello?' I called out softly, easing my way a few steps closer to her, not wanting to startle her too badly.

My best efforts failed, regretfully. She jumped in an exaggerated manner, trembling from the shock. Once she saw me, however, she relaxed.

'You were at the docks, in London,' she blurted by way of greeting.

'As were you,' I replied, coming up beside her.

'You... You work with Sherlock Holmes,' she said, wagging her pointer finger at me in a rather incredulous way.

My cheeks reddened slightly at her words, and I was very glad for the lack of light. 'I don't work with him,' I said, denying my plainest ambitions. 'I'm just Doctor Watson's half-sister. I came to stay with them following the loss of my family.'

'Then what on Earth were you doing at a Scotland Yard crime scene?'

'I've been wanting to ask you the same thing. The West India Docks hardly seemed the proper place for a girl of your appearance to be going for a stroll, much less unaccompanied.'

'I've never been one to follow rules. Observing the different social classes fascinates me. When they function with so little, it makes me wonder why we have so much. We keep a home in London, and we travel there every time Father has business to do in the city and can find someone else to supervise the mines in his absence. That used to be Simon.'

'Well, next time you go for a stroll in the lower classes, you'd do well to dress to blend in more.'

'Anyhow, you're one to tell me that my presence in the docks isn't proper!'

'I can't disclose specifics. It was a political matter, and was only last month. A diplomat was kidnapped and held for ransom. His aide got too cocky in attempting to organise an exchange on his own and was killed at the docks.'

'So, you did work with Sherlock Holmes on a case!'

'In a manner of speaking, yes.'

'What connection did that man I saw have to all this?'

'He worked for the man who organised it, setting up a scheme to turn our government against a fragile ally.'

There was a pause, and then Nicole said meaningfully, 'I don't know why you don't think you're working with him.'

'Because I'm only a girl, and such a thing would be highly irregular.'

As I spoke, I considered my choice of words. *Holmes has a troop of Irregulars. He seldom deals in regular occurrences.*

'But he allowed you to come here with him and the doctor. You could have been instructed to stay in London; I'm sure there's a housekeeper of some sort who could mind you. No, at the very least, he's not excluding you from the investigation.'

She was, of course, entirely correct, and I did not realise it until she said so. Although Holmes' exterior was perfectly controlled, perhaps he was a little less reticent than usual concerning me. My heart jolted as I remembered what Lestrade had said to me about this very subject:

'None of us have ever seen him like this… I think it would be better if you heard the truth from him.'

I had dismissed my being taken along as being the result of John's worry for me as he had expressed it to Holmes yesterday, but the idea of it being more because Holmes trusted me caught me more than a little off guard.

Suddenly, a bell rang from somewhere in the house, cutting our conversation short. Nicole sharply turned in the direction of the stairwell.

'That'll be dinner,' she said. 'Come on, we'd best get downstairs before we're late.'

I noticed the tremors in her hands again and I made a mental note to ask her, perhaps sometime after dinner.

27

By the time dinner was over, the rain was pounding harder than ever. Mr Camberwell made no offers to entertain us after the meal, nor, I think, did any of us expect him to. Holmes and John wandered off, hands in their pockets, deep in conversation, and I went straight back to my room.

I was nearly done folding my clothing when there was a knock and Nicole entered.

'I'm sorry,' she said, her cheeks flushed a delicate, rosy pink. 'I don't mean to intrude. I just wanted to apologise on behalf of my father. My mother's passing was very hard on all of us.'

I watched the girl's face as she spoke. She wasn't telling me the truth. It wasn't her mother's death that had made her father so callous.

'My own mother passed away a few years ago as well, and it turned my father into a very secluded individual. Please, come in.' I gestured for her to sit down on the bed.

She obliged, closing the door softly.

'I thought you said earlier that you had lost your family,' she said softly, looking at me curiously through large brown eyes.

'I did,' I said with a sigh, setting down the stack of folded clothes and taking a seat beside her. 'My father – stepfather, I mean – was killed two months ago. After that, I had no family left and I was forced to leave my family's estate for London to stay with my half-brother, the only relative that I knew of. It came as a great surprise to me that he lodged with Sherlock Holmes.'

John was not the only family I had left. There was Ariana. God help her, if she was still alive following the brief glimpse I got of her before Moriarty took her again. I felt myself starting to shake, and I willed myself to control it.

'You mean you didn't know?' Nicole asked with a laugh.

'I knew of him, but no, I didn't know that they were in any way acquainted,' I replied, bringing myself sharply back to the present and resolving to enjoy the conversation.

Nicole grew dark and silent for a moment. When she looked up again, I could see fear in her eyes.

'Do you think you'll be able to find my brother?'

I reached over to place my hand on top of hers. 'No case is too formidable for Sherlock Holmes.'

'But he's been missing four days now. We have had no word from him and no idea of anywhere he could have gone.'

'What about the school friends you mentioned?'

'What of them?'

'Do you think they could have had anything to do with it?'

'No, of course not! They've been wonderful friends with Simon since he was at Eton years ago.'

'Nicole,' I said to her cautiously, 'your brother's friends were the last to see him, as far as we know. They're the first people Holmes is going to suspect as having arranged his disappearance.'

'They couldn't have.' The girl shook her head vehemently, biting her lip. Tears began to well up at the corners of her eyes. 'Simon's dead, isn't he? It's been four days and we've heard nothing. He can't still be alive, right?'

I wanted nothing less in that moment than to tell her so, but she was most likely correct. Four days was far too long a time to go without having heard anything. If he'd been staying somewhere else, he would have either returned home or sent word. If he'd been kidnapped, a ransom note would have been sent by now. I wasn't the only one who thought so. I'd seen it in Holmes' eyes when he read us the letter, and again on the train. He knew the odds as well as I did – better, even. He knew that in all probability, we were not coming to investigate a disappearance.

We were coming to investigate a murder.

I couldn't bring myself to say any of this to Nicole, fragile as she seemed, so I merely told her:

'There's always hope.'

The doubt and insincerity in my words must have carried, for the fear and emptiness in her eyes did not desist. As we sat silently on my bed, listening to the sounds of the storm outside the window, I wished I could do something more to help her hold on to an anchor, whether it was to be lifted to a less desolate and hopeless place.

Chapter 4: All That Lives Must Die

Thou know'st 'tis common; all that lives must die,
Passing through nature to eternity.
— William Shakespeare

The next morning dawned a pale grey. Most of the clouds from the day before had moved out, leaving only a thin veil between us and the sky. The rain had stopped, the only reminder of it being a fresh scent on the verge of overpowering the bitter taste permanently hanging around the mines. Puddles dotted the lawn every few yards as I peered out one of the windows on either side of the front doors after breakfast.

Holmes and John had donned thick rubber boots to search the woods we had driven through the afternoon before. It was probable, Holmes had said, that if anything had happened to Simon Camberwell, any clues would be in the forest, since he would've had to pass through it to return home.

I should have been out there, searching as well. I had lost something very dear to me too. Every time I closed my eyes or allowed my mind to stray, I felt the pain. Having my twin, the other half of my soul, ripped from my side left a hole in my heart that couldn't be filled by anything else. And God help me, I would save as many other people from feeling it as I possibly could. Never mind what was proper. Even if I was a lady, I was still a human, and I could still do as much – probably more than – most people cared to.

Biting my lip, I turned to Nicole, who was standing pale-faced behind me. 'Do you have any extra pairs of boots?'

She nodded immediately, almost eagerly, as if she'd been waiting for me to say something. 'Yes, I believe they're in the kitchen. The servants use them when crossing the lawn to walk into town. I'll go fetch them.'

She returned a few moments later, clutching two pairs of boots – one for me and one, as it would seem, for her.

'Wait,' I said, holding out an arm. 'You should stay here.'

'If you're going out there, then so am I.'

'Nicole, there could be things you don't want to see,' I warned her, thinking of the fearful look in her eyes the previous night as she'd realised that her brother may be dead. 'I am more accustomed to these things. I would not be living with Sherlock Holmes if I couldn't handle it.'

Nicole looked up at me, eyes wide. 'I can see what's in your eyes, Emily. I can see the pain, the fear. You're not living with Sherlock Holmes because you can handle it, but because you don't have a choice. And yet still you don't shy away. You don't hesitate to dive in. A part of you wants to run, yet you don't. I will not stay away from it either. Let me come with you.'

Her words hit me like a physical blow. I drew back, inadvertently giving her enough room to finish donning her boots.

Yet there was something about it; something that I couldn't draw away from, no matter how much it hurt. I wanted to help, to save people.

Healers, my mother had called those who knew pain and had a burning desire to help others through it.

You're a healer, Emily, she had told me. *And Ariana is a fighter through and through. But there is more fight than you think in those who heal. The battle against despair is the toughest of all.*

I swallowed hard and pulled on my boots. 'Let's go, then.'

We silently slipped out the door and set off across the lawn, pulling the collars of our cloaks up against the chill breeze.

'Bad luck with the storm last night,' I muttered as I sidestepped a puddle only to land in a deeper one.

'What do you mean?' asked Nicole, taking note of my wrong step.

'Water is the bane of the investigator,' I replied, quoting what I had heard Holmes say earlier this month after he returned from a case in St. John's Wood. 'Water cleanses. And the worst thing that could happen to a crime scene is that it could be cleansed. It washes away most vital evidence. Footprints, a blood trail, a scrap of cloth, all of it could be gone unless we're very lucky. After last night's storm, I fear the trail could by now be cold.'

'There's still hope, though?' Nicole asked with a shudder as the breeze picked up slightly.

The dead leaves on the trees rustled as we approached the woods.

'If there is, it's slim. Not even Sherlock Holmes can outsmart the forces of nature.'

As we kept walking, the trees loomed above us, menacing even in full daylight. The air seemed to get damper and colder, and the bridge of twisted branches over our heads seemed designed to keep some evil tucked away inside, and I knew that whatever the forest was keeping hidden, we had entered its territory.

'Keep your eyes peeled,' I said to Nicole, my voice low.

As I spoke, I let my own eyes sweep over the area around us, concentrating on every leaf and patch of mud that covered the ground, looking for anything out of the ordinary.

'Emily,' called Nicole after about ten minutes. 'What on Earth is that stench? Is that coming from the mines?'

Something was odd. Nicole had lived here all her life. She had doubtless wandered these woods many times. She knew what odours came from the mines.

I sniffed the air. I hadn't noticed it before. All my focus had been trained on my sight, not my sense of smell. Nicole had done well pointing the smell out. I raised a hand to cover my nose and mouth, feeling bile rising in my throat.

The smell was awful, worse than the bitterness of the smoke and exposed minerals coming from the mines. It was worse, even, than the foul odour of waste, filth, and unwashed bodies that pierced every street of London. It was the most nauseating thing I'd ever smelled, like the sickly-sweet aroma of rotted fruit, but somehow different. Somehow worse.

Even though I was shielding my nose and mouth, my eyes watered still. I was terrified to breathe in. How couldn't this be smelled from all over the forest?

Nicole and I, both trying to breathe as little as possible, looked around frantically for the source. I tried desperately to blink the tears away so I could see the ground in front of me in something other than brown streaks. Suddenly, from somewhere off to my right, Nicole screamed.

My heart pounding, I whirled around and started running in her direction. Standing in the middle of a web of protruding tree roots, stretching to meet each other in a dark, twisting embrace, the girl stood deathly still and stared at something laying between two trees.

I heard shouting in the distance and knew that Holmes and John had heard us as well. Nevertheless, I moved closer to see what she was staring at, transfixed.

Oh my God.

A body, mangled and torn, in the process of decomposing. As a rule, everything breaks down over time when exposed to the elements. Especially the human body. After what was presumably four days, the skin was turning a sickening shade of marbled green, and starting to sag, no longer connected to the skeleton. The eyes were larger than normal, bulging out of the sockets with the expression of a madman. The jawbone was tense and rigid, the mouth clenched tightly.

I turned away for a moment to swallow the bile. When I turned back, I saw Nicole collapsed onto the ground, still screaming at the top of her lungs, her entire body shaking. I knelt and tried to speak to her, to comfort her, but my words did no good. Her body was rigid with shock. I wasn't strong enough to pull her away from her brother's decaying corpse.

A moment later, Holmes and John arrived, and they too briefly covered their faces in reaction to the smell. They barely glanced my way.

'Watson,' Holmes said in a low voice, 'kindly escort Miss Camberwell back to the house. I'd like your opinion as a medical man when you return.'

My brother nodded and gently lifted Nicole in his arms. I listened to her hysterical wailing fade as they disappeared into the trees.

I didn't think Holmes would acknowledge my presence, but he turned his full attention to me as soon as our companions were gone.

'What are you doing out here?' he asked sharply.

'I-I needed to help search. I couldn't just stay there.'

I expected him to let a quick, half-smile flit across his face, with some remark about how he knew and that was why he'd let me come along, but instead he just gave me a cold and hard look. 'What was *she* doing out here?'

I averted my gaze to the ground. 'I know I shouldn't have let her come. I tried to warn her. But she wouldn't allow me to leave her behind.'

Holmes did not reply this time, but instead sprang down upon the ground and whipped out a small magnifying lens, shuffling through the mess of leaves.

'Staggering footsteps led from the direction of the town,' he muttered under his breath. He abruptly sprang up to examine the bottom of the dead man's shoes, then, apparently satisfied, returned to his examination of the ground.

'Excuse me,' I said, watching his actions carefully, 'but wouldn't all the rain last night have washed away any footprints?'

He didn't reply, too caught up in studying the evident marks underneath the blanket of wet leaves.

A few moments later, John reappeared and immediately knelt to examine the body.

'Dilated pupils,' he muttered softly to himself. He lifted the arm to look at the fingers. 'Advanced cyanosis and *rigor mortis*. Holmes?'

Holmes looked up. 'Yes, old fellow?'

'The cause of death appears to have been asphyxiation. The way the jaw is clenched indicates advanced *rigor mortis*, which could be the result of convulsions and seizures prior to death, and there are scrapes on the knuckles which suggest that he was grappling for something – My God!'

John recoiled at something on top of the body. Holmes sprang over, eyes alight with the thrill of the hunt. My brother pulled out his handkerchief and used it to gingerly pick up an object. Despite the stench and repulsing sight before me, I took a few steps closer and leaned in to look. I gasped and raised a hand to cover my mouth again.

'Oh my God, is that his tongue?'

John replied without looking up at me, working to pry the dead man's mouth open. 'Yes, it is. It must have been convulsions, then. So severe that he bit off his own tongue.' Only then did my brother do a double take. 'Emily, what the blazes are you doing here? Go back to the house. Stay with Miss Camberwell.'

I crossed my arms and shook my head, attempting to steel myself against the malodour. 'Absolutely not. You did not force me to stay in London, I expect because you didn't trust me not to get in trouble, so you can't expect me to just sit around here, especially when there's a case – one that you let me hear about from the inception. I'm staying right here, and you'd do well to include me.'

John sighed and muttered what seemed to be a prayer, but did nothing to desist me as he continued to examine the body.

Gingerly, I stepped around to kneel behind the corpse's head, moving my eyes slowly over the body, my mouth tightly closed to keep from gagging.

'What's that?' I asked, pointing to a tear in the shirt covering the late Simon Camberwell's left shoulder.

'Probably nothing but the markings of an animal that came by looking for old flesh to eat,' said John, giving the area nothing but a brief glance.

Holmes, however, shook his head, looking very interested.

'No, not an animal, Watson,' he exclaimed, bending over the shoulder. 'An animal's claws or teeth would make a jagged tear as they ripped it apart. This wound is too straight-edged and clean.' He took a small knife from the pocket of his trousers and began cutting away at the cloth with it until the entire area of the shoulder was exposed. 'Halloa! What have we here?'

John and I both leaned in to have a closer look. There was a shallow wound in his shoulder, about an inch long. A small amount of dried blood was crusted on the cloth.

My brother furrowed his brow in confusion. 'A knife wound... But it's hardly a scratch. Remarkably shallow. It couldn't have hit any major arteries. Not enough blood loss to cause much harm. And how on Earth could it have caused asphyxiation like that?'

'Asphyxiation, you say?' Holmes looked from the man's eyes, pupils enlarged, the tongue he had bitten off in thrashing about before death, to the wound on the left shoulder studiously.

'Yes, Holmes,' said John, watching him as if trying to conclude the purpose of his methods. 'From the lack of scabbing around the wound, I'd wager it was sustained no more than four hours prior to his unfortunate demise. But that coupled with the asphyxiation doesn't add up.'

'Perhaps the wound was sustained in that fight he had with his friends, and the asphyxiation was brought about by alcohol poisoning. We know he'd been drinking,' I suggested.

Holmes gave me a sideways look, nodding slightly, giving me the smallest of grins.

'Excellent hypothesis, Emily, but no,' he said, gesturing to the corpse's mouth. 'Alcohol poisoning was not a factor in the asphyxiation here. Note the lack of frothing around the mouth. You are correct about one thing, though: the wound was sustained during the altercation outside of the public house in town.'

'Then what of the asphyxiation?' John asked.

'My dear fellow, it only doesn't add up when one has a distinctive lack of imagination. You must consider what may be true, furthering what you already know for certain. The knife certainly must have been tipped with poison of some sort, causing the convulsions and death by asphyxiation.'

John shook his head. 'But with a four-day old corpse and no weapon, how will we ascertain which poison?'

Holmes had leaned back upon his knees and scoured the area around us with the sharp gaze of an eagle. With a cry, he sprang up and ran about ten yards to a pile of leaves. A moment later, he gave an exclamation of triumph and held up a silver and ebony pocketknife with his handkerchief.

John and I both dashed to see what clues the Great Detective had uncovered.

My brother gaped at the knife. 'But how can that be? If the wound was sustained in the fight outside the pub, how the blazes did the knife get here? Suppose one of the others drew their knife during the altercation and lightly slashed him across the shoulder to keep him in check. The knife would have stayed in their possession. But somehow it ended up in a pile of leaves several yards away from a dead body.'

An elated expression on his face, Holmes turned over the knife, crusted with dried blood, and held it out so that we could see. The initials *S.C.* were engraved into the ebony handle.

'It was Simon's knife,' John said.

'But how does that explain how it came to be buried under the leaves?' I asked.

'And how did you know it would be there?' John added.

'The former cannot be answered as yet. The latter, however, I can elaborate upon. You will observe this tree here.' He pointed to the tall tree that loomed above us. 'I have made a study of the deciduous trees of Britain, and even written a little monograph on the subject. This is a *Sorbus aria,* or a common whitebeam. And this is a leaf of the common whitebeam.' He stooped to pick it up and display it to us. It was small and round, with jagged edges shaped like tiny teeth. 'So, it seems more than odd that the leaves of the *Quercus robur,* or the English oak – one of which is growing a few yards away – should be found directly underneath the common whitebeam.' He picked up another handful of leaves, which bore the familiar curved shape of oaks.

'Simply absurd,' John muttered, shaking his head.

'I do believe,' said Holmes, pocketing the dead man's knife wrapped in his own handkerchief, 'that once the proper authorities to move the body have been notified, a word with the owner of that public house is in order.'

Chapter 5 : The Test of Courage

Often the test of courage is not to die but to live.
– Vittorio Alfieri

Rosedale Abbey seemed even more silent and sinister in the hours leading into that night than it had when we had arrived the day before.

Holmes had headed into town to notify the constabulary that there was a body in the woods and then speak to the proprietor of the pub.

In the meantime, John had gone to Nicole's room to check on her. I stood in the doorway while he took her pulse and looked in her eyes.

'She's in shock,' he told me, pulling the blankets further up around the girl. 'Stay with her, please, and come fetch me if there are any worrying changes. I'll be in my chambers.'

Nicole was curled up on her side. She didn't stir or speak for hours. I simply sat, watching her, plagued with the memory of her brother's body.

I'd never seen – or smelled – a corpse that old. *Death has a smell*, my mother had taught us. It was musky, like mouldy cloth and dust. *For death*, she had said, *is as old as life*. When the reaper came, you couldn't distinguish his presence as more than a feeling or a shadow, and he left that scent behind him.

I had smelled death in my mother's chambers on the day she died, but the scent emanating from the corpse in the woods was different. It wasn't a subtle odour, bitter-tasting and hanging thick in the air like a veil. It had been a putrid, nauseating odour, far different than anything I had ever experienced.

In need of a distraction, I raised myself off my perch at the edge of the bed and went to sit at the small desk in the corner. I pulled out a sheet of paper from one of the drawers which stood halfway open, dipped a pen into the open inkwell, and began to write.

10th October, 1887

Dear Andrew,

I must confess that this place is much darker than I expected it to be. The trees loom out of the ground like tall, armoured guards shielding some cruel secret. There are mines nearby, and they emit a bitter scent that permeates all the surrounding earth. It is so pungent you can taste it. It leaves a harsh aftertaste when you breathe in or open your mouth. It's less strong here at the Abbey, but it is still present.

Simon Camberwell is dead. We found his half-rotted body this morning, in the woods between the house and the town. My God, it was the worst thing I've ever smelled. It's worse than the slums, worse, even, than the mines here.

I didn't say anything to you when we spoke prior to our departure, but I knew from the time Holmes read the letter what was going to happen. I knew that three days was far too long. I knew that if he were still alive, the family would have heard something. Holmes knew it too. I saw his face on the train. I saw it as soon as I walked into the sitting room to hear the contents of the letter. It was true, of course.

Nicole, the one who wrote to us, was the girl at the docks when we were investigating the small matter of that red X. I knew I remembered her name, but I couldn't recall where from until she greeted us on the lawn.

And then there's the matter of her father. Mr Camberwell and Nicole are now the only two members of the family living in the house, as far as I can tell. I have a suspicion that he hurts her. She hasn't said anything about it to me and I'm hesitant to ask.

North Yorkshire truly is a dismal place, especially near the mines. I only wish that there was something to lift my spirits and tear me away from the oppression of such a dark and fearsome landscape.

Just then, Nicole spoke, her voice quiet and sounding much like a frightened mouse.

'Please don't go.'

'What was that?' I put the pen down and moved to sit on the bed beside her again.

'My father will want you to leave now that you've found Simon. Please don't.' Her lip quivered.

I put a hand gently on her shoulder. 'Nicole, your father is the authority in this house. We can hardly stay without his permission. But that doesn't mean we still won't find who murdered your brother.'

She shook her head, her breathing coming fast. 'No, please. I can't stay in this house without Simon. He's the only one who could hold my father back.'

With her words came a weight that dropped in my stomach, and I knew that my intuitions about Mr Camberwell had been correct.

'He hurts you, doesn't he?' I asked softly, already knowing the answer.

Nicole nodded, whimpering as she tried and failed to hold back tears, subconsciously jerking her arms closer to her body, as if to shield them.

'May I see?' I asked, holding out a hand.

It took her a moment, but then the girl haltingly held out her left arm to me. I carefully pushed up the sleeve of her dress.

A knot formed in my stomach when Nicole bit her lip as I uncovered an arm riddled up and down with bruises of various sickening colours. Older ones fading to yellow with a tinge of blue, and newer ones, black and purple, coupled with small scrapes. Some in the shape of fingerprints, others from blunt objects.

'I'm going to fetch John,' I said, starting to stand.

'No!' she said sharply, taking hold of my arm with the hand she'd extended to me, hissing from the pain of the effort it must have taken her to grip.

I bent down close to her. 'Nicole, please. He's a doctor. He can help. Not only that, but surely intervention as far as your father is concerned is required.'

She seemed incredibly doubtful and more than a little anxious at the prospect, but she let go of my arm.

Absently stuffing the unfinished letter to Andrew into my pocket, I hurriedly left the room and knocked on my brother's door. He hastily answered, and I knew he'd been expecting me to come for him – a fact confirmed by the black medical bag I could see sitting ready on the bed.

'What's changed?'

'She's alert and speaking. But it's something else. Bring your bag.'

He followed me back to Nicole's room, where we found her sitting upright, her arms folded in her lap. John cursed under his breath when he saw her arm. From the way the air suddenly changed in the room, I knew that he had guessed where the mottled bruises had come from. I could see Nicole shaking as she held up the arm for John to examine, and she was unable to look either of us in the eye.

'Miss Camberwell, may I see your other arm?'

Biting her lip and keeping her eyes focused on the sheets, the girl nodded and raised her right arm, pushing up the sleeve to reveal more bruises. At the sight of them my stomach turned again, and the most predominant among my feelings was a horrible, heartbreaking pity for what she must have gone through. Worse, undoubtedly, than the hardships I had faced during my own youth. My stepfather, though decidedly hostile, had rarely interacted with Ariana and I, let alone laid a hand on us.

As John began to stick plaster bandages over her scrapes and rub salve carefully onto the bruises, he asked, 'How long has your father been doing this to you, Miss Camberwell?'

'Has it been since your mother died last year?' I asked, if only to gauge her reaction. I remembered the look in her eyes when she had dismissed that as the cause of her father's callousness the night before.

'No, since before that. Ever since I can remember, really.'

Something had begun to tug at the corners of my mind, the answer to some mystery that lay just beyond my reach. Mr Camberwell's violent tendencies, Mrs Camberwell's death a year ago, and the pictures that had been recently taken down from the walls. They were all connected somehow, but this was not the moment to plumb the affair.

John set his jaw firmly, and in that tiny fraction of time, I saw something of the war in him. It was rare that these glimpses showed through his wizened exterior. I supposed that must not always have been the case. He had come home from Afghanistan six years ago, he had told me, sent back to England following a gunshot wound in the shoulder and a bout of enteric fever. Not long after his return, he began lodging and taking cases with Sherlock Holmes, dragged back into war probably sooner than he would have liked.

The war against crime was different than that against the Ghazis which had raged in the last decade, but it was no more civil and no less perilous. I knew that memories of what my brother had seen still haunted him, but when one is accustomed to fighting, one does not let weakness take hold in fear of becoming a less effective soldier.

I swallowed hard, realising that I had let weakness take hold within myself. My arms itched at the very thought. I squeezed my eyes closed and vowed to be strong. John was not the only one in the middle of a war. I was there too. And God help me, I had already vowed not to retreat; I would devote my efforts to helping people. I was a healer. And healers were most needed on the front lines.

Opening my eyes, I saw John closing his bag and straightening up.

'I'm going to see if Holmes is in his room,' he said, giving me a sideways glance. 'Emily, if you see him, tell him I would benefit from a word with him.'

With my nod of understanding, he left.

I turned to Nicole. 'Do you wish me to stay with you?'

She shook her head. 'No, it's quite all right. But, before you go, I'd like to know something. Does Holmes suspect Simon's friends from Eton?'

Her words made me pause. I sank down on the bed beside her. 'At this point in the investigation, it's a likely path to follow. They were, as far as we know, the last ones to see your brother alive, and they fought prior to his death. There were also some… indications around the area of his… person today.'

I chose my words carefully, not wanting to upset her.

Nicole looked up at me sharply. 'What sort of indications?'

'Are you sure you want to know?'

She took a deep, steadying breath. 'Yes, I'm quite all right. I am not afraid of death, just of the harm the living inflict.'

Her voice was stronger than it had been since we arrived. This was the girl who had been wandering the West India Docks, who knew more than a little about defending her virtues and wasn't afraid of a bit of blood.

'Your brother, it seems, was slashed across the shoulder with his own pocketknife.'

'Isn't that a little odd? He wouldn't have done it himself.'

'The presumption is that during the altercation outside the pub, he threatened one of his friends with it, and they took it from him. Then he perhaps said or did something provocative, and the one who had taken his knife either slashed him in contempt, or to keep him in check.'

Nicole closed her eyes for a moment, obviously recalling the sight of her only brother's body. 'He didn't bleed to death, though. So, what killed him?'

'Poison. We aren't sure what sort, though.'

Suddenly, Holmes appeared in the doorway, looking out of breath.

'Where's Watson?' he asked urgently.

47

'He said he was going to look for you in your room, but I imagine he's back in his own chambers by now. What did you find so worth the rush?'

'Perhaps the answer to no less than a fourth of our mystery. Come, now. The game is afoot!'

Chapter 6: The Dim Haze of Mystery

It is the dim haze of mystery that adds enchantment to pursuit.
— *Antoine Rivarol*

I rose from the bed and ran out the door to follow Holmes in hopes of keeping up, for he had moved so quickly that one could have missed him in a blink.

The door to John's room had been thrown open in haste and I skidded to a halt in the doorway. Holmes was standing beside my brother's desk chair, bouncing on the balls of his feet. I saw the familiar glint in his eye that always marked the discovery of some great thread of the yarn that had to be followed to its source.

John looked up from a manuscript in front of him. Holmes' sudden arrival seemed to have startled him; there was a rather sizable splatter of ink on the page which seemed to distress him greatly.

'She's here, Holmes, get on with it! Whatever can have caused you such great excitement?' My brother asked, gingerly setting down his pen on top of the desk blotter.

'The proprietor of the public house in town, an establishment known as the Black Kettle, was very useful indeed. He told me the details of the altercation he witnessed between Simon Camberwell and his associates several days ago. It was a drunken spat, not very soundly based, as they'd all had a good number of drinks.

'The late Mr Camberwell took his ebony handled knife from his pocket and waved it threateningly in the face of Edward Jamison, one of his friends. Mr Jamison took the knife from Mr Camberwell and when he attempted to wrest it from his grip, slashed him across the shoulder with it as a warning. Mr Camberwell then grabbed his knife and staggered off in the direction of the woods, heading home. The owner of the Black Kettle, one Mr Peter Johnson, then followed Mr Camberwell a short way into the woods to ascertain that he would not be any danger to himself. He was staggering in a halting sort of way, cursing to himself and punching tree trunks in his drunken haze.'

'That explains the scrapes on his knuckles,' I interjected.

Holmes snapped his fingers. 'Indeed it does. Mr Johnson admitted to me that Mr Camberwell seemed too violent, and he didn't dare to approach him. He began shouting at things which weren't there and soon tossed his knife down upon the ground in a fit of rage, looking about him as though he were being hunted and tossing handfuls of leaves on top of the knife. He wandered so far off the path that eventually Mr Johnson ceased his efforts and returned to town.'

'That certainly offers some help in determining the poison,' John mused softly.

'Does it, though?' I asked. 'We know he was drunk. Couldn't that behaviour have just been the influence of the alcohol?'

'But you said poison killed him, so doesn't that seem like the more plausible explanation?' came a voice from the doorway, perfectly calm and level.

I whirled around to find Nicole leaning in the doorway, arms folded thoughtfully in front of her chest.

'Miss Camberwell, what are you doing out of bed?' John asked.

'Including myself, seeing as no one else seems entirely keen to do so.'

Holmes and John both turned to glare at me as if I were the one responsible for giving our young client the idea to jump into the midst of the investigation of her brother's murder.

Was I? I couldn't be sure.

I most definitely hadn't stopped her from accompanying me into the woods. But I also wouldn't have been able to. Brute force would certainly not have been proper, and she was as strong-willed and independent as myself. I decided that it hadn't been my fault and wiped any semblance of guilt from my mind.

'I understand your reservations on the matter of allowing me to assist in your investigation,' the girl continued. 'It would be unethical to allow the client – someone emotionally involved – to put themselves in a harrowing position. You must also have your doubts concerning the fact that I am a girl with no practical experience in the field of investigation. But I assure you that I can be of more help than anyone else you will find here.

'This is a mining town, and the locals are of a significantly lower class than us. They are all very suspicious of anyone well-dressed, seeing as they are accustomed to rather unpleasant and demanding aristocracy wielding such clothing. I'm sure you witnessed that reticence, Mr Holmes, when you went to speak to

Mr Johnson. Everyone else around the bar immediately left, did they not? And didn't old Johnson require more than a little prodding before saying anything to you? It's less than likely that my father would offer you any assistance. I am your best option.'

Holmes and John seemed more than a little taken aback by her bold speech.

'She's right, you know,' I said. 'You saw the way the coachman looked at us when we arrived. Those of our social status are far from welcomed here. Our options are few, and quite frankly, if we don't accept her offer, we'd be better off giving up the case altogether. And you know we can't do that, for the *integrity of justice*.'

I had my eyes fixed largely on Holmes, knowing that he would never be capable of giving up an active investigation. He prided himself on his successes far too much for that.

Finally, after a moment of silence so pronounced that I could almost hear the gears grinding in Holmes' head, he spoke, his face devoid of any emotional inclination.

'Fine. But not for any reason other than that this place is her home, and she is far more knowledgeable than we are.'

Somehow, I was not filled with triumph, having successfully defended Nicole and secured a victory for this investigation. Something had been tugging at my mind since the girl had said that her father was unlikely to offer any assistance. His disposition made it unlikely that he would not eject us from the house once he received news that we had uncovered his son's body. Did he even know?

I turned to Holmes and John. 'Did either of you inform Mr Camberwell of his son's demise?'

'I did inform him of it, yes,' John said. 'It was when I brought Miss Camberwell back to the house today. He stopped me and asked what had happened.'

'Don't you find it a little strange that he didn't demand that we leave the premises by nightfall? He made it explicitly clear that we were only to stay until we found his son, within the week.'

Nicole nodded. 'That's true. He most certainly would have demanded that you head back to London by now.'

John shook his head. 'All I know is that he called for a housemaid to bring tea to his room, then walked away.'

Something was amiss. Even if the man had needed some time to compose himself after receiving the news, surely by now we would have heard something else, whether it was an order to leave or not.

There was a change in the air. I turned to Holmes, sensing that the scales of logical probability were at work in his mind, weighing various scenarios against the facts and narrowing down the list of the most probable candidates for the truth.

'Miss Camberwell, where is your father's room?' he asked, snapping back into the present.

'It's on the next floor down. He wanted it close to his study, rather than on the same floor as the other bedrooms. I'll show you.'

I thought for a moment that Holmes would object, in an attempt to shield Nicole from whatever we might find, but evidently the situation was too urgent, for he nodded and darted for the door. John, Nicole, and I had no choice but to follow him.

Mr Camberwell's door was locked when we arrived downstairs. Holmes cursed under his breath as he rattled the doorknob.

'Mr Camberwell!' he shouted. 'Open the door!'

There was no reply.

He cursed again, looking around us quickly for anyone who might have a key to the room, but the hallway was empty.

'Stand back,' he growled, and immediately John pushed Nicole and I back a few paces.

Holmes aimed a strong and well-placed kick at the lock, and the door swung inwards. On seeing what was inside the room, the detective gave a cry of dismay and ran inside, John close behind.

I moved forward as well, though I had a little more than a sinking feeling about what lay inside the room.

Nicole gasped and her hands flew up to her face, but her reaction was far less anguished than it had been this morning.

The body of Mr Camberwell lay on the floor, looking as stiff and pale as his son, though much less green.

John knelt on the floor, feeling at the dead man's neck for any semblance of a pulse, but it was, of course, futile. Even I knew, from the way that his eyes were glazed over, that there was no possibility of his life being spared.

My eyes travelled from the rigid corpse to the sheets that appeared to have been aggressively pulled from the bed to the teacup that had been dropped on the carpet, spilling its contents. And even before John proclaimed it, I knew that the cause of death was the same as that of Simon Camberwell. Asphyxiation. I knew that the same poison had killed both father and son, which meant the same person was to blame.

But as Nicole stood beside me, trembling in shock and fear, I wondered who could have wanted both Camberwells dead. And what of the remaining family member who stood beside me – was she next?

Chapter 7: We Are for the Dark

The bright day is done,
And we are for the dark.
— William Shakespeare

John advised Nicole to leave the room several times, but she would not.

'I have nothing to fear from the dead,' she said, softly but firmly.

I knew that neither man was inclined towards removing her, so the girl was allowed to remain, although her presence was entirely ignored. Not knowing what to do, she remained motionless just inside the doorway, purposely averting her eyes from the body of her father, rigid and frozen eternally in the act of some grotesque seizure or convulsion.

I dared not say anything, but Nicole's continued presence was doing no good to the process of searching for clues, and it was obviously an act of sheer stubbornness on her part. I understood, of course. I had been both curious and stubborn enough to discreetly slip into the first crime scene I had seen, the victim also in my case being my own father. Similarly, Nicole wanted not as much to help examine the scene as to prove herself worthy of helping in other areas of the investigation.

After only a few moments of searching the room, during which he had lowered himself flat to closely study the area of the carpet soiled with the spilled tea, Holmes sprang to his feet.

'There are scuffs of mud on the carpet by the door. There are two teacups, although Mr Camberwell's was the only one to be used. Someone was here, not long after we returned to the house. Someone from outside, familiar enough to be seen in the bedroom rather than the study. Someone who was offered tea but refused because he knew it was poisoned. Nicole, who is familiar enough with your father? Who could have been here?'

The girl looked from the second cup sitting pristinely on the tea service to the scuffs of dried mud in the square shape of a man's toe. Her mouth was agape in wonder and confusion.

'I haven't a clue.'

Holmes let out a breath, affording a glance at the corpse. 'This isn't just a simple murder anymore. Two are dead. This is a far more serious case than I had previously anticipated. I'm going to send a telegraph to Lestrade. Perhaps he shall be kind enough to come up and assist us. We may have need of a warrant by the end.'

He departed the room after this announcement, leaving me with a very sinister feeling.

Holmes was correct. One murder was something I knew he had solved many times before, with assistance from the local constabulary. But multiple murders made this far more serious. Even the Great Detective knew that he couldn't properly take on that kind of an investigation without the proper authorities. The risks were far too high, especially when we now had to protect someone who seemed a likely candidate for the next target.

My gaze snapped to Nicole. 'May I speak to you outside for a moment?'

She nodded, seeming more willing to listen to me than the men, and followed me as I gestured towards the open doorway. The hallway was quite refreshing; less oppressive than the bedroom had been where the presence of a horrifically positioned dead body added considerably to the foul atmosphere.

I took a breath. 'Nicole, your father and your brother are both dead. You are the only surviving member of the family.'

She ducked her head, fidgeting with the sleeve of her dress. 'You think I may be the next target,' she said softly, shivering and glancing behind her.

'I think that it is a definite possibility. And we must watch your every move so that we can avoid you being poisoned as well. I want you to be prepared for that. And I must ask, is there anyone that you know of who has reason to want your family out of the way?'

The girl shook her head slowly. 'Most of the workers in town hate us, but they don't seem… capable, if you know what I mean.'

'So, you don't believe any of them would be able to commit premeditated murder?'

'No. I doubt they would have the capacity for murder at all. They may not appreciate our class much, but they're very passive.'

I nodded, and was about to reply when she added, 'Although…'

'Yes?' I prompted her, raising my eyebrows.

She bit her lip, seeming indecisive for a moment before speaking: 'There have been a rather unusual number of fights among the townsfolk of late.'

'Unusually high?'

'Very. The past few months, there have been far more reports of violence in the town than there have been in years. Especially among those working in the mines. But I still doubt any of them would have enough anger to kill. The worst casualty has been a few broken bones, as far as I've heard.'

'We're going to find Holmes,' I said, not wanting to waste a second more. 'I can't risk any harm befalling you.'

'Didn't he go into town to send a telegram?'

'Most certainly not. He'll have sent one of the house staff into town to send the message. The constabulary will need to be alerted as well. He wouldn't leave the scene alone for that long. Not while any evidence is still fresh.'

I grabbed Nicole's arm to pull her along with me and set off down the hall. We found the detective standing in the foyer, hands clasped behind his back and tersely waiting for the return of whatever messenger he had sent and help from the local constabulary, which I doubt consisted of more than one or two officers and a local doctor.

'Holmes, Nicole – er, Miss Camberwell, sorry – has some information for you.' I nodded at her. 'Tell him what you told me.'

She took a breath and confidently repeated, word for word, everything about the townspeople and the recent violence.

'That's very interesting, oh, very interesting indeed,' Holmes exclaimed, seeming very passionate about having new information. I wasn't sure just how important it was, but I knew that it must tie in somehow.

'Holmes, what of the poison? It's likely that it was consumed through the tea, is it not?'

'It is indeed.'

'Does that mean you'll be able to identify it?' Nicole asked.

He gave her a sort of look as if he was still slightly annoyed with having to answer her as more than a client, but spoke all the same:

'Once the assistance from the town arrives, I shall take a sample from what is left, and I will do whatever tests I am able to perform in order to identify its identity and origin.'

'Will Lestrade come?' I asked.

'I suspect we shall have an answer to that question by morning,' Holmes replied, giving yet another glance towards the window, clearly hoping to see the light of a lantern being held aloft as the carriage containing the town constabulary rolled in.

'But in your opinion, will he come?'

'As I have often told Watson, Lestrade is the pick of a bad lot. Over the years I have worked with Scotland Yard, he has formed a sort of dogged loyalty to me. And he is by far the most sensible and intelligent of the Yarders. It would take a great deal indeed to keep him in London when I have promised him multiple murders in a small, secluded mining town. Yes, he will come. Now Emily, why don't you escort Miss Camberwell up to her bedroom? It is late, and likely these next few days will not be easy ones. You would both do well to get some rest.'

I nodded and took Nicole's arm, turning to lead her up to her room, but stopped.

'Nicole, why don't you go on up? There's something I wish to discuss with Mr Holmes. I'll only be a moment.'

The detective gave me a stern look, probably for dismissing his precaution of keeping an eye on her at all times. Meanwhile, Nicole looked at me sceptically, but I nodded to her and she turned and walked up the stairs. As I watched, I could see that she did not tremble as she did so. Her father was gone. And however terrifying it might be to have a murderer targeting her family, she was safe, at least from her own blood.

Once she was out of sight, I turned to Holmes. 'Are Simon Camberwell's friends from Eton still your main suspects?'

'There's no reason for them not to be. They were the last ones to see him alive, and—'

'No, they weren't.'

'Pardon?'

'According to what the pub owner told you, he was the last one to see Simon alive.'

A thoughtful look crossed over Holmes' face. 'This is true… But Johnson – as far as we know – had no motive to kill either of the men. Young Mr Camberwell's friends, however, were seen fighting with him just hours before his demise.'

I fixed my eyes on the floor for a moment before raising them again to look at Holmes. 'Have you any plans to speak with them?'

'I would prefer to wait until Lestrade arrives, in the event that proof becomes available, and an arrest must be made. Now please, see to it that Miss Camberwell stays safe. Do not lead her into danger. Surely you are already aware that she may be the next target.'

'I am. And I have alerted her of that fact, as well. Goodnight, Holmes.' I turned grimly and ascended the stairs, keeping my shoulders tense, for I knew that relaxation would dull my senses.

'Please stay with me tonight,' Nicole had pleaded, and I had not had it within me to refuse. It was my duty, not just because Holmes had ordered it, but because she had just lost everything she'd known. I knew her fear all too well.

I was sitting on the edge of her bed, as apprehensive as ever, but this time not without reason.

60

Something was wrong. Nicole was perfectly calm as she obliviously gave a monologue about her family history, but I wasn't listening. My eyes were focused on the scuff marks on the windowsill. There were also little clumps of mud visible on the floor underneath.

Someone had come in that way.

Is that how they had entered the house?

What if they were still here?

My breath came quicker. My eyes flitted around for other indications or signs of movement before finally falling on the folding doors of the closet. They were partially open.

In that moment I could have sworn I saw the sharp glint of an eye caught in the lamplight.

In another instant it was gone.

Stop talking, I willed Nicole.

But instead, I let the silence in the rest of the room drown out her voice. I could hear a sound.

Heavy breathing.

Was it coming from the intruder stashed in the closet or were they my own panicked breaths?

My senses were rife with danger. With each heartbeat, the feeling coursed through my veins, sending a tingling shock into my fingers and toes.

I reached out and grabbed Nicole by the arm, letting instinct take over my actions, and was vaguely aware of her abruptly stopping in the middle of a sentence.

'Emily, what—'

I didn't reply. If there was indeed someone hiding in the closet, I didn't want to confirm that I knew they were there.

Casting a warning glance in her direction, I quickly opened the door and pushed her out of the room.

I lingered in the doorway. My first thought was that we should run and get help. John and Holmes' rooms were just down the hall. By now they would both be in bed.

No. If we both left the room, the intruder would escape through the window with no chance of us discovering who he was.

So, I turned to Nicole and hissed, 'Run.'

She stared, wide-eyed, for a moment, but didn't question me. And she seemed to understand the hidden meaning in the word, for she immediately turned and ran down the hall.

I did not stop to watch. Andrew had taught me well and I had enough confidence to handle a brief encounter. I took a breath, strode to the closet door, and wrenched it open.

I did not recognize the face inside, nor did I have time enough to think about it, for immediately something was clasped over my mouth.

My stomach turned.

It was sweet. Horribly sweet, like rotting fruit.

Everything in my head turned to mist. My eyes flickered closed, and all I could see around me was utter darkness.

Chapter 8: The Coward's Weapon

The coward's weapon, poison.
– John Fletcher

It must have been some hours later that I awoke. Slowly, I became aware that I was lying in my bed at Rosedale Abbey. My brother, Nicole, and Holmes were all in the room.

Light was streaming through the window. It must have been morning. God, it was bright, and my mind still felt fuzzy.

I tried to open my mouth to speak, but immediately John was pushing a glass of water in my face, taking my pulse and looking closely at my eyes as I drank.

'How do you feel?' he asked.

I looked from Nicole, who was looking on anxiously, to Holmes, who was leaning on the wall by the door nonchalantly. Judging by the surreptitious glances he kept sending in my direction, he was trying not to show too much concern but failing miserably.

'My head hurts,' I replied, carefully forming the words, 'but other than that I'm all right. What happened?'

'I found you on the floor after Miss Camberwell came to fetch me,' explained my brother. 'She said she didn't know what had happened, only that you had made it clear that she was to come get me. Chloroform wouldn't keep you under for this long, but it was definitely some sort of strong sedative. It could have been a much worse reaction considering your injuries earlier this year.'

I forced myself upwards, batting away my brother's protests, and put up a hand to massage my temples. After a moment, bits and pieces of the previous night came back.

'There was an intruder in Nicole's room,' I said haltingly. 'He'd come in through the window and was hiding in the closet. I think the window was how he'd entered the house in the first place, to poison Mr Camberwell's tea, without attracting notice at any of the doors. He must have then left the house and returned as a guest of Mr Camberwell. He must have been looking for something; he could have escaped at any point while we were distracted.

'I didn't think anything of the mud by the doorway because I thought John tracked it in when he brought Nicole back from the forest. When I noticed the patterns of it, I told Nicole to run, then I opened the closet, and then...' I trailed off, for my mind could not produce a single detail after.

'And then what?' Holmes prompted eagerly, face shining at the knowledge that I must have seen the intruder's face. 'What did he look like? Did he say anything to you? Watson, hand her paper, she can sketch him!'

I looked down at my hands, folded neatly on my lap, shaking my head. 'I... I don't know. I can't remember the face.'

'Well, I'm sure you can! Was it narrow or round? Did he have a short or long nose? What colour were his eyes?'

'Holmes!' my brother barked.

The detective snapped his mouth closed.

'Short-term retrograde amnesia is common with many sedatives and anaesthetics,' John spoke in a more even tone now. 'We're lucky she remembers as much as she does. Do not push the limits of her brain.'

'I do apologise, Emily,' Holmes said, softer.

I nodded at him. 'It's quite all right. I'll certainly let you know if I remember anything.'

Morning. It was morning. What seemed so very important about morning? I closed my eyes, thinking for a moment.

'Lestrade,' I murmured under my breath, turning to Holmes. 'Have you had an answer from Lestrade?'

'It was brought to me less than half an hour ago. He said that he would be more than happy to hand off his cases to another inspector and that he'd be here by nightfall, with a warrant he can serve if necessary.'

Nicole gave him a sideways look from where she was perched delicately on the plush stool in front of the bureau. 'Aren't you going to tell her?'

I looked at them through slitted eyes, the peculiarity of this statement shooing away the remainder of the fog in my brain. 'Tell me what?'

Holmes looked rather sheepish, refusing to lift his gaze from the vicinity of the worn edges of the carpet in the doorway. 'Watson was attached to your side in case of your awakening, and my experiments required an extra set of hands.'

'We know what the poison is!' exclaimed Nicole, her eyes shining with a light I had only seen in her when she walked up to Andrew and I at the docks.

'Last night I took a sample of what was left of the late Mr Camberwell's tea,' said Holmes. 'I observed from the stain on the carpet that what he was drinking was of the black tea variety,

Masala Chai, to be precise. Its preparation is quite singular, in its true Eastern form. You see, the leaves must be—'

'If you have written a monograph on the preparation of this tea, I'm sure we can all read it another time. Please, shorten your explanation. Emily is quite in need of some rest.' John sounded incredibly short-tempered.

'I've just had hours of rest; I don't need more!'

'Anaesthetisation is not the same as *rest.*'

I wasn't all that surprised at my brother's mood. If what Holmes had said was true, he had been awake watching me all night.

The detective sighed and continued his story, sans the tea-making process.

'The oxidised leaves from which the tea is made are of a distinct earthy colour. However, a handful of the ground leaves left in the bottom of the cup were very different, a peculiar shade of dark green. So, I procured a sample of the powder and took it back to my chambers to conduct a few preliminary tests.

'The poison that was the cause of both deaths was a member of the *Solanaceae* family. *Atropa Belladonna,* more commonly known as Deadly Nightshade. It grows plentifully in a number of damp, wooded areas throughout Europe. You might spot clusters of them in these very woods, were you to look. One leaf from the plant is fatal within a few hours, and poisoning causes the same symptoms which we have been able to deduce that both of our victims experienced. Sensitivity to light and blurred vision would be the first symptoms to exhibit themselves, followed by loss of balance and a staggering gait, leading into hallucinations, slurred speech, convulsions, and finally death, caused by spasms so severe that the respiratory system becomes rigid and unresponsive.'

A chill went through me as I was afforded a clearer mental image of the process of death, fitting in the description Holmes gave with the story Mr Johnson, the pub owner, had told him.

'Does this help narrow down possible suspects?' I asked, trying to shake the dismal picture from my mind.

'If you are wondering if I have cleared the young Mr Camberwell's school mates as suspects, the answer is still no, and will remain so, in my opinion.'

'But you haven't even spoken to them,' Nicole protested. 'Once you do, you'll see that they are not capable of something like this.'

'Miss Camberwell, I only form my opinions based on what the current evidence tells me.'

I furrowed my brow in surprise.

John froze in the act of reaching for something in his bag.

One point that Sherlock Holmes was fiercely adamant about in the field of investigation was that one should never, in any circumstance, form an opinion, a theory, or a judgement before having all the evidence. And having not yet gotten the stories of his prime suspects and some of the most important witnesses, he certainly did not have all the evidence.

Something was rotten in the county of Yorkshire.

John hesitantly pulled his hand back, folding his arms across his chest and turning fully towards the detective.

'Holmes,' he asked cautiously, 'are you all right?'

'Quite fine, old fellow,' he responded, although sounding quite distant. Without another word, he straightened up and walked briskly out of the room.

'...Am I missing something?' Nicole looked back and forth between the two of us with raised eyebrows.

'Holmes has a habit of telling us never to form a hypothesis without first holding all the cards in our hand,' I explained, my eyes still fixed on the hallway. 'It's the only piece of advice that he stresses so… persistently.'

'Then why on earth did he just attempt to defend an unfounded theory?'

John shook his head. 'I have absolutely no idea.'

Sherlock Holmes was, despite all his eccentricities, a creature of habit. Whenever we were lacking a case, he took trips to the British Museum every Friday at two o'clock to study their anthropological specimens and do whatever reading he liked in their private library.

He also kept to the same schedule of sleeping unless he was actively investigating a case. He always played the violin when thinking through the evidence in murder and forgery cases, and always smoked his pipe on robbery, domestic, and political cases. The pipe always depended on the day of week and the weather.

From eight o'clock to eleven o'clock every morning, he devoted his time to reading the dozens of London newspapers he was subscribed to.

It took nothing short of a figurative explosion to throw the Great Detective off his self-made routine.

The morals to which he clung were very clear cut, it was doubtful there was anything which could blur the line between black and white in his mind. Something must be very wrong for him to completely disregard one of such morals.

A fog was rolling in over the moors and across the lawn as I mused about this irregular attitude. As the mist crept ever closer, it swallowed everything in its path, until all was blurred and distorted in shape.

I began to feel shaky, my eyes suddenly drooping. John had been right. I did require more rest. I stifled a yawn and sank into my desk chair, too weary to stand.

Some time later, a light shaking on my shoulder woke me up. I started despite the heaviness of slumber still lingering.

The face that I saw was not who I had expected. Cropped hair overdue for a trim and an instantly identifiable smirk.

'Andrew?' I half-exclaimed and half-queried, suppressing a yawn.

'Good evening to you too.'

'What in heaven's name are you doing here?'

He shrugged. 'I was passing by Inspector Lestrade's desk last night and saw he had a telegram from Sherlock Holmes. I was, of course, concerned about you, seeing the mention of multiple murders. So, I bought a ticket on the only train coming to North Yorkshire today and rode up with Lestrade.'

'So, you weren't invited?'

Andrew snorted softly. 'Heavens, no. Don't be ridiculous. I seldom require an invitation to make up my mind.'

I couldn't hold back a giggle as I stood up to more properly greet him. 'It's very sweet, you know,' I said, reaching out to embrace him.

He enclosed my waist gently in his arms and pulled me closer to him. 'Yes, I know,' he murmured.

I let his warmth surround me for a moment before I pulled back to study his face.

'Were Holmes and Lestrade pleased to see you?' I asked, already knowing the answer.

'Lestrade told me I should have stayed in London, and Holmes told me I wasn't qualified enough to be here, and it was bad enough that he already had to involve two girls. Oh, about that—'

'You met Nicole?'

'Yes, she was downstairs with Holmes and your brother to greet us. What was she doing at the West India Docks?'

'All I'm going to say at present is that we're kindred spirits.'

Suddenly a thought struck me. I backed out of his embrace.

'What is it?'

'Andrew, none of them know about us. Aren't they wondering why you're here?'

'Well, I can't say that I think any of them would be especially surprised,' he admitted. 'And from the curious look Holmes gave me, I'd wager that he's already deduced it.'

My face darkened as the reality of the situation swept over me once again, and the excitement of unexpectedly seeing Andrew was washed away. I sank slowly onto the bed.

'This family is being targeted. Both the father and son have been poisoned.'

'Poisoned?' Andrew's eyes lifted in alarm.

'Yes. *Atropa Belladonna*, Holmes deduced. Andrew, I'm frightened,' I confessed. 'Nicole might be targeted next, and something's wrong with Holmes. He's not himself. He's not—'

Andrew stopped me by placing a finger to my lips.

'Shhh,' he drew me closer. 'It's all right. Poison is the weapon of cowards, you know. Those too scared to get their hands dirty. They can cause pain and death without soiling their hands and watching the light go out in their victim's eyes. The danger is not as great as it would be in the case of shootings or stabbings. This killer is not to be feared. We can use this against him.'

70

I knew that Andrew was right. But he was also wrong. The killer wouldn't come out in the open. But that didn't necessarily make it easier to catch him. He was a silent killer, as fluid and dark as the shadows. He might be anywhere.

If anything, his secrecy made him even more dangerous.

Chapter 9: Present Fears

Present fears are less than horrible imaginings.
– William Shakespeare

The fog did not lift as the day went on – it only got thicker. Soon enough, nothing could be seen, not even the misguided shapes that had been there before. Everything was shrouded in a grey, oppressive mist, floating over us like some ghost drawn evermore to places beyond our reach.

The butler and cook – husband and wife – were shaken, but seemed resolved to stay as long as any Camberwell lived in the house.

There being a larger number of us, we filed into the drawing room after dinner instead of immediately retiring to our chambers.

'Miss Camberwell, did your father have a will?' asked Lestrade, who was pacing near the hearth with his hands in his pockets.

'Not that I am aware of,' she said quietly. 'He had no affections, and much of his time was poured into the mines. Everything else was pointless to him. Even his own family.'

'What was his motivation for investing so much in the mines?' Holmes asked. A glint was in his eye, but somehow, I was afraid to look upon his face for more than a second.

'I couldn't say,' replied Nicole, shaking her head. 'My grandfather was the one who first owned the mine. It's been my father's ever since my grandfather died a few years before I was born.'

'How did he die?' I wasn't quite sure what made me ask. Something was nagging at the back of my mind, about the mines and the violence among the townspeople.

'Consumption, I was told,' Nicole answered, looking at me with curiosity in her eyes. 'Why? Is that important?'

'I doubt her late grandfather had anything to do with all of this, Emily.' Holmes waved away the thought.

Lestrade stopped his pacing precipitously. It didn't take any great leap of logic to realise that he had noticed that something was amiss with the detective as easily as we had.

'Holmes...' he started, but did not make any move to finish the sentence. His brow was furrowed in suspicion.

'Do make some effort to complete your sentences in a proper grammatical fashion, Lestrade. Kindly don't leave us hanging.'

This alarmed the inspector even more. As I shifted my gaze to John, I could see that he was just as shocked. While Holmes occasionally slighted Lestrade and the other Scotland Yarders, he never lashed out verbally. Something was truly amiss.

From the sharp intake of breath beside me, it was obvious that Andrew now realised it too. I was thankful for his epiphany.

His shushing of me earlier when I tried to tell him had not been comforting in the least.

John gave the detective a look that was normally reserved for when he returned from investigations in the middle of the night with blood dripping down his face.

'Holmes, you are not acting like yourself. Might I suggest that you retire early tonight? Miss Camberwell has lost her family, and they must be buried within the next couple of days. Your attitude is not helping her grieving process, nor your own investigation.'

Holmes gave my brother a piercing look and rose from his seat, departing the room with the grandiose drift adopted by so many birds of prey.

'What the devil's the matter with him?' Lestrade huffed.

'We haven't the foggiest idea,' I offered. 'But it is not something we can simply ignore until it passes. He's holding onto biased theories as well.'

A vacant expression had crossed Nicole's face. She suddenly whispered, 'It's the mines.'

'Pardon?' Lestrade asked, his eyes narrowed in confusion.

I could all but see her consciousness slowly drifting back into the room. She took a deep breath, pulling her sleeves down further, not meeting anyone's gaze. Instead, she looked into the glowing embers of the fireplace.

'It's nothing.' While the girl's tone was enough to convince the others, I looked into her eyes and knew that it was not true. Something was bothering her deeply, but this was not the time to ask.

'I think it's obvious that Holmes' investigative skills are suffering at present, for whatever reason,' I said instead. 'But that does not change the fact that there is a killer on the loose who will not be brought to justice while he has his sights set so stubbornly on Simon Camberwell's friends. I think we should launch an investigation without him.'

'You jest!' Lestrade laughed incredulously. 'We can't possibly solve it without the Great Detective's help.'

'I'm sure we can do something to that end, at least,' John piped up in support. 'Scotland Yard does it, so I am sure that we can do just as much.'

This elicited another laugh from the Inspector.

'Doctor Watson,' he said gravely, 'we at the Yard hate to admit it, but our success record without Mr Holmes is dismal indeed. We can't do a whit without him.'

'That doesn't mean *we* can't do it,' I pointed out. 'For goodness' sake, Lestrade, you've known Holmes for how long?'

The man furrowed his brow and counted off on his fingers. 'Why, nearly ten years now!'

I turned to my brother. 'John, you've lived with him for how many years?'

'Six,' he returned promptly, not even blinking. He had obviously already been thinking of this, for he did not even hesitate a fraction of a second.

'And I may have only been acquainted with him for a little under two months, but I've picked up a great deal, and I was no stranger to logical reasoning balanced with intuition before coming to Baker Street. Nicole isn't dull in any sense of the word either. And Andrew? Regardless of what you say about his experience and qualifications, Lestrade, he has spent just as much time as you soaking up the police environment. None of us are imbeciles. There's no reason we can't do this.'

'There is one stipulation,' John noted after I was finished, crossing his arms and casting a glance towards the door as though Holmes himself may be eavesdropping on our covert conversation.

'What's that?'

'Holmes can't under any circumstances know that we're investigating without him.'

'Well, how in God's name can we expect to be able to keep that from him?' Lestrade asked, a harsh and disbelieving tone in his voice. 'He's bloody Sherlock Holmes. If he can tell by a scuff on a man's finger the last time he was out gambling, then sure as hell he'll know we're conspiring behind his back.'

'I have a lot of experience watching dealings with diplomats,' Andrew said, speaking for the first time. I turned to see him leaning casually against a panel of carved bas relief depicting what appeared to be the Spanish Armada. His hair wouldn't lay flat, as usual, and he had obviously long ago abandoned any attempts to discipline it.

Something about his quiet and relaxed demeanour made my stomach churn lightly as if dozens of butterflies were fluttering around inside. It caused a warm feeling to spread all throughout my abdomen and chest cavity. I quickly averted my eyes, for fear the bubbling heat rising inside me would flush my cheeks.

'Go on,' I nodded to him instead, trying to dispel what had come over me.

'Often our government will be required to withhold certain information from foreign dignitaries with whom we are liaising; not for any malicious purpose, but because we are protecting them or ourselves. By doing this, they are involved, but we play a different hand when they're not looking.'

Nicole cocked her head in confusion. 'But I get the impression that Sherlock Holmes is always looking.'

I knew exactly what Andrew was trying to say.

'Holmes is affected by something,' I said in response to her statement. 'He's far less conscientious than usual. What Andrew is saying is that Holmes needs to feel as if he's in charge. Of course, he won't be as suspicious if we keep him where he's comfortable. We let him lead, and we follow. He won't notice anything amiss in the background because he's accustomed to dismissing anything below his deductions.

'That leaves us free to commence an investigation of our design. Trying to butt heads with him on his theories won't cause anything but more friction. If we just let him think whatever on earth he's thinking, we'll be free to take our own courses of action.'

I shivered as I said this. I may have been unorthodox in my levels of independence, but I too was accustomed to being under Holmes' lead on cases, however few I'd been involved in so far. This was different from what I had encountered in the Moriarty and Ivanov cases. In those instances, I had a rather painful suspicion that Holmes knew exactly what I had kept from him, though whether that was any fault of mine, I would probably never know. This time, he must not know. As strange and foreign as the feeling seemed at the time, I feared what would happen if he did.

I knew Nicole was not in her room. I had been on the verge of drifting into some semblance of sleep when I heard the creak of what could only have been her door across the hallway. Seconds later, soft footfalls moved towards the stairs to the ground floor.

Alarm shook every part of my mind. Whether or not Holmes' judgement was logical and trustworthy, he had still placed Nicole under my protection. He had trusted me with her life.

Her sneaking out of her room and off to some unknown place in the middle of the night was certainly not safe in any regard, especially considering that an intruder had been far too close for comfort only last night. Then again, she was a kindred spirit of mine; I knew that in her place, I would do the same. A bit of space to breathe and release from omnipresent constraint trumped a risk of being murdered. Especially when said risk felt too surreal to truly be anything of this world.

But a desire for space did not change the fact that her experience in protecting herself from harm was scant at best. Nicole wasn't even aware of the dangers of wearing upper class clothing into the slums.

I tossed back the covers and got out of bed, pulling a candle and match from the desk in the corner. After wasting a precious moment fumbling with the candle holder and match, I had the candle lit and cautiously left my room, letting the fluttering flame guide my way down the dark and still unfamiliar hallway.

Slowly, I made my way to the stairs. A door squeaked open. I started so much, I feared my candle might snuff itself out. In the dim light, I could barely make out Andrew's ruffled hair. He appeared to be in a nightshirt and had hastily pulled on trousers underneath.

'What's going on?' he whispered, sounding even more groggy than me.

'I'm not sure,' I replied, suppressing a harsh shiver as a draft swept through the corridor, 'but Nicole just left her room and went downstairs. I'm going to make sure she's not in danger.'

'Where did she go?'

I was about to reply when another draft from behind me made me turn and look at the window. The night outside was as thick and black as fresh pitch. There were no stars or moon. The fog was still hanging over the land, cloaking everything in secrecy. I felt a strange pull begging me to be a part of the mystery.

And then I knew. It was intuition, not a guess.

'She's outside.'

The alarm left Andrew's face and was replaced by unbridled fear.

'Let's go,' he said, putting a hand on my back and gently guiding me down the stairs.

I was stumbling over the hem of my long nightgown. I couldn't move fast enough. With a glance at my feet, Andrew realised this and took my hand instead, taking the steps two at a time, pulling me after him.

I stopped him at the landing. 'Here, take the candle. I'll trip if I don't hold up my skirt.'

He nodded. I busied my right hand with holding up my nightgown. Satisfied, Andrew pulled me down the rest of the stairs and then towards the front doors. The air was far colder down here, where the floor was stone and continuous drafts from beneath the door seeped into the house.

I shivered but had no time adjust, for Andrew pushed the door open, dragging me out into the cold night air with him.

Nicole was sitting on the steps in front of the house. She didn't react when the door opened; only hung her head in disappointment that she'd been discovered so quickly.

'Nicole?' Andrew said to her softly. 'It's not safe to be out here. Come back inside with us.'

She made no reply.

I pulled my hand out of his grasp and descended the steps until I was right beside her, putting my hand gently on her shoulder.

'Nicole, Andrew is right. I'm supposed to be keeping you safe. We should go back inside.'

She lifted her head to look at me. The fear in her eyes was the sort you feel when you find yourself directly in the middle of your worst nightmare. When you find yourself in the midst of a battle you never wanted to fight. One you'd been running from for what seemed like an eternity. It was resignation. It was misery and impending doom.

'It's the mines,' she echoed her words from earlier this evening.

I turned to Andrew. 'Go on inside. I'll only be a moment.'

'Emily…' He looked wary, and rightfully so.

'Go.' I fixed him with a stern look. He knew better than to protest.

Once we were alone, I gingerly sat on the stone steps beside Nicole, wincing as the bitter cold met the thin cloth covering my body. Even though I could already feel the loss of sensation in my hindquarters, I did my best to ignore the chill.

'What do you mean, about the mines?' I asked her.

She drew a shaky breath, coughing as her lungs expelled the frigid air she had tried to inhale.

'There are stories,' she said finally, her voice hushed, as though some consciousness in the fog or the trees might be listening. 'The people in the town would never talk to me, but I was around enough to hear them talk. They said that something was disturbed when my grandfather first opened the mines. No one knows what, but they say something lives down there, under the Earth, and that it lay embedded in the rock for hundreds of years. I never believed it, but something killed both men who would have had authority to keep the mines open, and something's affecting Holmes' mind.'

I confess that I could not help but shudder at the thought of what she was saying. There were tales all over the world of spirits in the mines, but every logical part of my brain dismissed it immediately. Turning to face the girl, I took both of her hands.

'Nicole, I want you to listen to me. I know how hard this is. You've just lost all you had left of a family. But it was not some mere legend that did this to them. You heard what Holmes said, and you saw the results for yourself. It was poison that killed them. Monsters wouldn't have any need of poison, if I may so boldly say. This is the work of a mortal. You must focus on the logical scenario, the one far brighter and less terrifying. A monster, I doubt we'd have the resources to beat. But we *can* beat a killer.'

From the way Nicole gave me a shaky smile, it appeared that I had convinced her, at least temporarily. Now if only I could convince myself.

I helped her stand and led her back to the door. But as I did, a thought struck me.

The legend Nicole had recounted to me told of something that wanted the mines closed. She was entirely correct when she said that the two men dead were the ones with the power to keep the mines open – the owner and his heir.

Someone did want the mines closed. And they were willing to kill to see it done.

Chapter 10: Divine Prerogative

Doubt, the essential preliminary of all improvement and discovery, must accompany the stages of man's onward progress. The faculty of doubting and questioning, without which those of comparison and judgement would be useless, is itself a divine prerogative of the reason.
– Albert Pike

The next day, Oliver and Simon Camberwell were laid to rest in a family plot a few hundred yards behind Rosedale Abbey.

The day was once again cool and grey, but the fog had lifted, and our line of vision was clear as we solemnly made our way out of the house to meet the wagon carrying the coffins. An unrelenting wind made the trees bow before us, as if in respect for the dead. From somewhere in the woods, a crow screeched, spurring at least thirteen others to echo it in unison.

I was glad that I had packed a black satin dress, for otherwise I would have felt very improper and out of place.

83

Andrew's hand rested on my back as the six of us came to stop at the base of a hill, where two fresh holes had been dug on either side of an already existing gravestone, which bore the name Mary Elizabeth Camberwell. The withered remains of a flower lay beside it.

Nicole immediately bent down to pick it up, tenderly cupping it in her hands as she returned to my other side. She took a steadying breath and squared her shoulders as the preacher from town opened his Bible. My brain could not focus on what he was saying, for upon observing the scene before me, I was struck with a thought.

I had not attended my stepfather's funeral. Certainly, none of the Moriarty brothers had attended it, therefore Ariana and I were the only people who could've been expected to. Had there been a service? Or had his body been dumped into the ground without any pomp and circumstance whatsoever?

It wasn't that it made any difference to me, especially not now. That was two months in the past, and as I had previously thought very much about, I had not particularly cared for my stepfather in any way. Not more than I did about any other person. As far as I was concerned, our mother had raised us, and he had merely given us a house in which to live.

He wasn't even my father by blood. I didn't *love* him. Not in the same way I had loved Mother. So, while I wasn't devastated upon realising that I had not been present at his funeral, it still felt wrong. He was not my real father, but he was still the one I had known for my entire life.

My hands shook as the flood of thoughts and mixed emotions made the healing scratches on my arm itch and ache.

I could feel Andrew's eyes on me. He gently and quietly took my hand into his, squeezing softly. Its presence made me feel complete, the tremors ceasing almost immediately.

The words of the priest flowed over me as he recited a final prayer over the coffins. Two men who I assumed had been summoned from the town lowered them into the ground.

Suddenly, there came a commotion from the woods. I heard branches snap. Something lumbered towards us. A flurry of crows rose from the ground and took off in all directions, frightened by the movement below.

A man ran into the clearing, jacket askew and out of breath. He stopped for a moment and stared at us. His eyes fell upon the coffins and he let out a cry, running forward until he was at the very edge of the grave.

We were so taken aback by this unexpected appearance that none of us said anything.

Nicole rushed to his side, taking his arm and trying to pull him back. 'Edward, step back, please.'

From the tone in her voice I knew that the grief she had been masking was breaking through. Edward, who must have been the friend of whom she had spoken in her letter, relaxed a little upon feeling the presence of her hand on his arm. He turned and embraced her tightly, closing his eyes and letting tears fall down his face.

'Miss Camberwell, who is this?' asked Holmes tersely.

John slapped him lightly on the arm, clearly attempting to convey that this was a most inappropriate moment, but he did not acknowledge it.

Nicole slipped out of the embrace, turning to us and wiping a single tear from her eye. 'This is Edward Jamison. He was my brother's closest friend from Eton. Edward, this is Sherlock Holmes. He's come from London with Doctor Watson and Miss Emily Watson to find out what happened to Simon. And that's Inspector Lestrade of Scotland Yard and Mr Andrew Lynch.'

'Sherlock Holmes!' Edward said with a weak laugh, composing himself quickly. 'By God, it's an honour! My father is acquainted with the Greens; I believe the wife used to be called Stoner, and she speaks very highly of you indeed, sir!'

The man stepped forward to shake Holmes' hand, but the detective only looked on with disdain until Edward backed off.

'Mr Jamison, how did you know that Simon Camberwell had died?' Holmes asked, suspicion tingeing his voice.

Andrew muttered some sort of prayer as he continued to keep hold of my hand. I was inclined to offer up the same sentiments, for Holmes was still fixated on the idea of one or more of Simon's friends being responsible for his death.

He might not be entirely in the wrong. How else could Edward have learned of Simon's death?

'I sent him a telegram, of course!' replied Nicole, and I exhaled in relief.

Holmes turned on the girl. 'You sent out information about your brother's murder? If he's the guilty party, Heaven knows what preparations for his escape he could have made!'

'He didn't escape; he rushed right to us!'

Edward's mouth fell open in shock.

'You-you think I was responsible for this?' he asked, anger and hurt in his voice. He gestured wildly at the grave. 'You think I had a part in putting my closest friend into a coffin? That I would do that to Nicole? He was like a brother to me, you bastard!'

Nicole hurriedly stepped in between the two men who appeared ready to throw punches. 'Gentlemen, please, I hardly think a graveside is the proper place for this!'

'She's right, Holmes, let's take this inside,' said John. There was a very clear warning in his voice. Were Holmes to speak out of turn again, he would regret it.

Holmes looked from John, to Nicole, to Edward, seething and defiant, before turning and walking stiffly back towards the house. Left awkwardly standing in his wake, the rest of us had no choice but to silently follow.

I glanced behind me at the edge of the woods, for I felt a strange sensation. It was the prickly feeling of eyes watching me. Indeed, I saw a shabbily dressed man of above average height peering out from behind a tree. There was something incredibly familiar to me about him. *What was it?* I was about to open my mouth to tell Andrew, who was walking just in front of me, but the face vanished.

But who was he? Why had I recognised him? I must have caught a glimpse of him when we arrived in town, I decided, turning to face ahead once again and trying to think nothing of it.

Edward Jamison wasn't tall, but he wasn't by any means short, either. His head rested a good three or four inches above Andrew's, but he was far shorter than Holmes. His hair was red and held itself stubbornly in a curly mop atop his head. His eyes were bright and sparkling with curiosity about the world, and he spoke in a most educated way, sounding extremely interested in things he did not know and equally passionate about everything that he did know.

'What kind of experiments usually help lead you to a killer?' he asked Holmes during dinner.

I examined Holmes' demeanour with bated breath. Edward was very eager to intrude upon his methods, and this was exactly the sort of thing which Holmes detested – especially when he was already in a foul mood.

'Mr Jamison, I am not pleased about your presence. I do not wish to disclose my methods to you at this time.' He stopped to eat a forkful of food, then continued. 'Now, I trust you'll be staying in town overnight and will return to your own place of residence in the morning?'

'Mr Holmes, I thought Nicole would have informed you. I'll be staying here.'

Holmes rapidly turned to the girl. 'Not possible. His name has not yet been cleared. Having any suspect under this roof is a potential danger to you.'

Nicole stiffly straightened in her seat, hesitating only a second before meeting Holmes' eye with a ferocious glint.

'I believe I am now the head of this household,' she said firmly. 'If I say that Edward stays, then he stays.'

'Miss Camberwell, you are under our protection,' protested Holmes, tossing his napkin down onto the table. 'It is our duty – my duty – to eliminate any potential threats to your safety.'

'No matter what you say, Mr Holmes, no matter what sort of grand delusion you're under, Edward is not a threat to me. You are not a god. Sometimes you are mistaken. Edward stays. I will not discuss the matter any further.'

A hushed silence fell over the table. After a moment, Holmes pushed back his chair and stood, his plate of food only half finished. 'I shall be excused. I have a murderer to catch, and much thinking to do.'

'Is he always so… stubborn?' asked Edward after the detective left, and although his voice was hushed, it still retained the eager and entirely intrigued air with which he had spoken everything since recovering from the shock of seeing his best friend's coffin.

I had to admit that his general attitude was slightly getting on my nerves.

'No,' replied John with a sigh. 'He most certainly is not. I must apologise for his shortness. He hasn't seemed himself these past few days.'

'Does anyone else here believe that I was responsible for Simon's death?'

'Not in the least, Mr Jamison,' I responded quickly. 'We spoke about it following one of Mr Holmes' outbursts. I for one can say that your reaction at the funeral today was genuine. I've been lied to a great many times…' I paused, carefully considering whether to say that I had also done a great deal of lying. I didn't. '…and I know what a rehearsed or fabricated reaction looks like. It takes a lot of experience and the right kind of person to tell a lie that passes inspection. If you'll allow me to say so, you most definitely are not such a person. That grief was the indubitable truth.'

Edward nodded, muttering his thanks. It was obvious that Holmes' suspicion was making him more than uncomfortable, as it left him without his continuous air of enthusiasm.

'Perhaps you can help us, Mr Jamison,' said Andrew softly, pushing back his empty plate.

'Help you with what, Mr Lynch? We have already established my innocence. I do not think there is much more I can do.'

'*We* have established your innocence, Mr Jamison. Holmes has not, and does not at present appear likely to,' John remarked. 'You may have realised that this greatly impedes the progress of the investigation. We are attempting to rectify this on our own. Holmes is not willing to give you a chance to tell us anything but how you did it. We are. We know that you didn't kill Simon Camberwell or his father. You were, however, one of the last people to see him alive.'

'We are willing to let you tell us your side of the story,' I interjected, giving John a sideways glance to make sure that he was not offended. He nodded, so I continued, 'In return, we will tell you everything we know, if that supplements any additional information. Do you think you can do that, Mr Jamison?'

He nodded rapidly. 'Most certainly. Anything to help find who did this to Simon. I... believe I've lost the remainder of my appetite. Shall we adjourn this to the drawing room, and you can tell me what you know first?'

'Certainly. But you will speak first, so that what we tell you does not unfairly influence it. We do not believe in your guilt, but we must make sure that the truth does not get muddled.'

Edward nodded his agreement, and we all stood. Nicole rang the bell for our plates to be taken away, and we silently made our way to the study through the door on the right side of the dining room.

'Mr Jamison, tell us what you remember from the night you last saw Simon,' Lestrade said, lighting a cigarette with a match from his pocket as we settled in our seats.

'Well, we'd all met in town – Simon, Patrick, Leslie, Victor, and myself – at the *Black Kettle* for a couple of rounds of drinks. We were discussing the deal from a few months ago—'

'What deal?' Andrew broke in, his eyes narrowed.

'You-you didn't know about it?' Edward asked in surprise.

We all shook our heads in unison.

'Please elaborate,' I prompted.

'About four months ago, the mines were in deep trouble. Wait, Nicole, didn't you know something about it?'

She lowered her gaze. 'All I knew was that both Simon and my father were very much thinly stretched for a time. Then you and the others came for a few days, and when you left, everything was all right again.'

'The funding for the mines was running out,' explained Edward. 'They could not find any of the ores. It had been nearly twenty years since they'd uncovered a major vein. They needed to dig deeper, but needed permission and money from the Government. Mr Camberwell had gone to Parliament, but they refused to give him more funding and equipment. He refused to tap into his own fortune, but they said he must come up with the money on his own. So, Simon contacted us. Mr Camberwell made us a deal. If we invested some of our money into the mines, he would split the profits made from the new ores with us.'

'And have those profits been worth the investment?' asked Lestrade.

'Very much so,' replied Edward with a nod. 'When they were digging, they uncovered a large supply of lead ore. It's very rare in its natural form, especially here. It could be sold to manufacturers for quite a high price.'

Lestrade looked between us. 'What do you think? A rival mining magnate?'

Andrew shook his head. 'No, these are family-owned mines. If a rival company wished to gain control, all they would have had to do was con Mr Camberwell into selling or offer him a higher price. Nicole, would your father have taken a higher offer than the profits he was making in exchange for the mines?'

Nicole gave a half smirk. 'Did my father seem like a sentimental man to you?'

'Let's take that as a yes. That's not a plausible reason for murder.'

'We understand the deal now,' I said to Edward. 'You can continue with your story.'

'As I said, we were meeting at the *Black Kettle* and discussing the deal we'd agreed to a few months ago and the profits we were already making from it. We had about four or five rounds apiece, then left the pub.'

'You were fighting outside,' said Nicole, a slight tremor in her voice. 'What were you fighting about?'

'It was mostly between Simon and I,' the young man admitted, fiddling with the lapel of his jacket. 'I will openly confess to you that we were all quite inebriated by this point. I had somehow come to the hazy conclusion that Simon was stealing a portion of the profits I was supposed to be receiving. We all disclosed what we were making, and my profits were somehow less. I do not recall how I concluded that Simon was responsible for this. I threatened him, and he pulled his own knife on me.

'I'm not quite sure that he knew what he was doing, not that any of us were completely in control of our actions to a certain degree, but he was waving the knife dangerously close to my throat. I took it from his hands, and he lunged, trying to get it back from me. I slashed him across the shoulder with it. I wasn't thinking. I was only trying to warn him to back off.'

The poison had been on the knife. Edward had slashed Simon with the knife. But he hadn't killed him. Had Simon himself put it on the knife? No, that couldn't have been it. He had no motive to kill Edward, or vice versa. So, who had laced the knife?

'What is it that you know?' Edward asked uneasily after a short time, looking at me with slight suspicion as I drew back with the gravity of my thought.

I shook off the urgency of the question that would put an end to our entire predicament and took a breath before answering.

'We know that both Simon Camberwell and his father are dead. They were both poisoned. Holmes has determined that the poison used was *Atropa Belladonna*. We believe...' I paused, debating if I should tell him about the knife, but ultimately had to

92

be candid with him as a courtesy for his own honesty. '...that in the case of Simon Camberwell, the knife you slashed him with had been coated in the poison.'

I knew at once that despite my morality, saying this had been a very unwise choice. The man lowered his head into his hands, rocking back and forth in internal agony.

John gave me a harsh look.

'Oh, God, I killed him!' Edward cried, gesturing at himself. 'Do you not see? I killed him! I slashed him with that knife!'

'You did not kill him, Mr Jamison,' John said firmly. 'You had no part in putting the poison there.'

'Then how the deuce did it get there?' Edward moaned.

John opened his mouth to reply, but I held up a hand. 'John, I think he has a point.'

'What?' John narrowed his eyes and cocked his head slightly, giving me a strange look.

'You can't possibly be reconsidering Mr Jamison as a suspect!' Lestrade said incredulously.

'Emily, we already established that it couldn't have been him!' Nicole exclaimed.

I heard Andrew inhale sharply beside me. 'No, she's right.'

'How *did* it get there?' I asked, repeating Edward's question. 'Well, the killer would have put it there, obviously. But how would he have known that Edward would slash Simon with it? That was an unforeseen circumstance. We could argue that Simon was not the intended victim... perhaps that Edward was.

'But again, how could the killer have foreseen whether Simon would cut Edward? It's impossible, unless Simon put it there himself. And that would be completely illogical, for Simon had absolutely no motive. If neither of them put it there, and the killer could not have predicted the way things would unfold, then perhaps the poison was never on the knife at all.'

'Well, then where the devil was it?' Lestrade asked.

'In his drink,' blurted Edward. 'It must have been.'

'Mr Johnson,' Nicole murmured. She looked up sharply. 'Do you think it was him?'

'But what would his motive be?' Andrew asked.

'He hates my family,' Nicole suggested.

'Nicole, I don't think your brother and father were killed because they belonged to this family,' I said, shaking my head. The suspicion had been in my head since I had spoken with her on the front steps the previous night. 'Someone wants the mines closed. They killed both the owner and the heir apparent. They weren't crimes of hate, but of revenge… or opportunity.'

'But why would Johnson want the mines to close?' asked Edward. 'He doesn't work there, he only owns the pub. If the mines closed, it would hurt his business.'

'Then maybe it's not him.'

'Who else might it be?' asked John.

An idea was milling around in my head, but I dared not voice it. Not in front of everyone. Especially not in front of Edward. I simply shook my head.

'I don't know, but it's late. We should retire. If we're all up late tomorrow, Holmes will be suspicious.'

Edward put up a hand. 'What's the matter with him, anyway?'

Before I could answer, Holmes himself appeared in the doorway.

'I thought I should inform you that I am going for a stroll,' he said in a patronising tone.

'Mr Holmes, pray tell, have you gone for any other strolls recently?' asked Edward before he could walk away.

94

'Mr Jamison, I fail to see the importance of such a question.'

I looked quickly at Edward's face. The glint was back in his eye. He was on to something.

'Holmes, answer the question!' I said forcefully.

The tone in my voice was enough to make him turn around in surprise. 'If you are so insistent upon knowing, yes. Two nights ago, I went out to clear my head and think the case over. That is why I was not in my room when Nicole came to report the intruder, and why she had to go on to Watson's room instead.'

'Mr Holmes, where did you go walking?'

The detective threw up his hands in exasperation. 'I still hold that this has no bearing on anything, but it was near the entrance of the mines. I was observing the equipment used in the digging and attempting to determine what was being mined.'

'It's lead ore,' replied Edward, his lips tight.

Holmes waved a hand dismissively. 'Yes, I know that! Pray tell me what your point is!'

'Lead ore is rare in its natural form. It is also highly toxic, as I am sure you are aware, Mr Holmes.'

'I am aware.'

'And symptoms of lead poisoning include but are not limited to impaired mental agility and an increase of violence and aggression,' Edward elaborated.

Nicole inhaled sharply. 'The workers in town!'

John took a hesitant step forward. 'And Holmes.'

Holmes let out an incredulous laugh. 'Don't be ridiculous, Watson! I have not been affected by the lead fumes near the mines!'

'Let go of the preposterous concept that you are immune to things that affect other people,' I admonished. 'Much as Nicole said earlier this evening, you are not a god. You are vulnerable. What Edward is saying presents a great possibility.'

'Lead exposure takes years to manifest symptoms! I am fine.'

Andrew shook his head. 'Not pure ore.'

'Stay here, everyone,' John muttered, walking briskly out of the room, pointing at Holmes as he passed. 'Especially you.'

He returned a moment later carrying a small glass containing water into which an off-white powder was quickly dissolving. He handed it to the detective.

'Drink this and retire to bed immediately. This should flush any effects of the lead out of your body, provided you help it along by resting. Now as Emily was saying before, it is late, and it would be a good idea for all of us to retire.'

Holmes downed the liquid with more than a little annoyance. Soon after, we were all ascending the stairs to our bedrooms.

Once I had readied myself for sleep, I was glad to feel the blankets encasing me and the pillow underneath my head. As sleep was beginning to overtake me, my overtaxed mind began thinking again of spots of blood adorning my arm, like a morbid pattern of lace against my fair skin. The still healing scratches on my arm began to burn with the thought, and as I curled into myself, I couldn't keep in a small sob. Hot tears oozed from beneath my eyelids until I was too tired to think anymore and was at last asleep.

Chapter 11: Not To Yield

To strive, to seek, to find, and not to yield.
– Alfred Lord Tennyson

The sun had barely started to rise when I was woken by a sharp, repetitive knocking on my bedroom door.

It was evident that I had been crying in my sleep: my face was damp and sticky, as was the pillow beneath me. I wiped my eyes with a shaky finger as I stood and shrugged on my dressing gown.

It must be Andrew or Nicole. They were the only ones who would have anything to say to me at such an hour. It must be something urgent; the tone in the knock betrayed that no time could be wasted. When I opened the door, it was neither of them.

The face of Sherlock Holmes greeted me. I groaned. Normally I would have kept such a reaction locked inside, but the hour was far too early for filters.

Holmes, already completely dressed, looked more alert than he had in days. I blinked, my vision blurred with sleep and tears, and looked him up and down.

'I take it that drink John gave you worked wonders,' I said at last, suppressing a yawn that threatened to escape as soon as I opened my mouth.

'Very much so,' he replied, almost jovially.

'Why in heaven's name are you in such a good mood?' I confess that I may have been glaring at him a little bit.

'Because Edward Jamison is innocent!'

I groaned again and collapsed against the doorframe, too tired to support myself in my exasperation.

'*Yes, I know.*'

He froze, cocking his head slightly. 'How do *you* know?'

'Because we spoke to him last night after you left. Besides, I knew it from the moment he first appeared at the funeral. That grief was genuine, though I'm not surprised you didn't notice it. How do *you* know?'

'I decided to test the blade of the late Simon Camberwell's knife to see if it had been rubbed with *Atropa Belladonna.*'

'It wasn't,' I said with a nod, turning to yawn into my hand.

'So *how* much exactly did you discuss last night?'

I held up a hand. 'Go ahead down to the drawing room, I'll meet you there to talk as soon as I'm dressed and powdered.'

Holmes nodded and left. I swung the door closed behind him, dropping my dressing gown on the bed and turning to the mirror.

A few minutes later, woken up considerably by the process of readying myself for appearance beyond my bedroom, I descended the stairs and found Holmes waiting in the drawing room. He was pacing in front of the hearth, a delighted spring in his step.

I sat down in the same place as I had the previous night, and told Holmes everything Edward had said to us, and everything we had theorised in turn. When I was finished, he sat down with his fingers steepled for a moment before replying.

'Why did this discussion take place during my absence in the first place?'

'Out of everything I just said to you, that is most certainly not the only comment I expected you to have.'

'It is only the first. But answer the question.'

'Because you were being unreasonable, and we realised that while your sights were set so stubbornly on Edward and Simon's other friends, progress on the investigation would not be stable, so we decided to pursue the matter further without you while it continued to be an issue.'

'All right, I can concede that point. I was being foolish and unreasonable, and I believe I owe everyone an apology. Next question. When can I speak to these other friends?'

'I'm sure they would need to be contacted first, or at the very least we would need to obtain their addresses.' I paused, remembering the thought I'd had the night before, wondering if I should share with Holmes, who had just recovered from an overly hard-headed loyalty to such a notion himself.

Investigations were not always about what was being considered for the first time. They did not demand new information. Much the contrary, for the same theories often had to be considered repeatedly from multiple angles until a solution was found. It did not matter that this take was not completely new. It needed to be shared.

I picked at a loose thread on my left sleeve as I took a breath. 'Holmes, about the other friends…'

'Yes?' he looked up with raised eyebrows.

'I was considering last night, after we looked at Mr Johnson as a potential suspect, if Simon's other friends might still be on the list? We know that Edward is innocent, but what about the rest of them?'

'I have spent the past several days in a hazy pursuit of such a solution, Emily, and I believe I have exhausted all possible angles.'

'That was then, but what about now?'

Holmes looked off to the side for a moment, his foot tapping errantly – a sure sign that he was deep in thought.

Finally, he turned back to me. 'What is your reasoning behind such a proposition?'

'It was Edward saying he somehow came under the impression that Simon was stealing from his shares of the mine profits. I thought that perhaps one of the others was doing such a thing, maybe that they wanted a larger share, and killing everyone else who would receive a share was the best way of doing so.'

'But you said that killing both the owner and heir to the mines means that they would close. What point is there if your share would be about to be cut short by your own murders?'

I stopped plucking loose threads from my clothing, my hands frozen in realisation, unable to articulate their own movements.

'That's very true. I also said that the motive for the murders must be wanting the mines closed.'

Holmes nodded sagaciously. 'And that is a very logical assertion. Very probable, in fact. That does considerably narrow down the list of suspects. Given the cards which we currently possess, that list does not include our victim's friends. Which is precisely why I wish to speak with them. Until we hold enough

100

of our own cards, we cannot effectively deduce what the other players hold in theirs.'

I couldn't hold back a smile. That was certainly the Holmes I knew, the logical thinker who never made a move before every possibility was planned.

'You're smiling,' he said, observing my facial expressions as some sort of novelty.

'Yes, I am. Why do you act so surprised by it? I am a human, I do have facial expressions which directly correlate to my emotions, you know.'

'It's simply that it's been some time since I've seen you smile like that, is all,' he said softly, once again trying to appear as if he were not watching me with great interest.

An uneasy feeling was starting to grow inside me, but I swallowed it and spoke:

'It's been rather a mentally taxing time for me, what with being kidnapped and catching a glimpse of my sister in such a fashion. I'm sure you understand.'

Holmes gave an almost imperceptible nod. 'Indeed, I do.'

Curiosity and a bit of unbidden anger rose up inside of me. What did he understand about the ordeal I'd been through? What did he know of the loss, the fear, the injustice that I felt? He was so logical, bordering on coldness at times. What could he presume to know about the enormous, tangled mess that was emotion, and how much more tangled it became after a traumatic experience?

I had to bite my tongue against letting out a sharp remark on the subject, forcing the thoughts out of my mind as a twinge of guilt reminded me that Holmes' past was as much of an enigma to me as the location of my sister. It wasn't that he didn't know what I had been through, more that I didn't know what he had been through.

I became increasingly aware of the fact that my shoulders were tense, a clear indicator of my discomfort with the potential directions of this conversation. In an ineffective attempt to undo the loss to my cause, I took a purposely deep breath and relaxed.

Holmes had noticed, of course.

'Emily, I am aware that you have been struggling since your encounter with Moriarty under less than domestic circumstances. The night terrors, the melancholy, your habit of withdrawing. When you came to us, despite what happened at your home in Suffolk, you were more energetic and focused. The climax of the Ivanov case changed you more than your stepfather's murder.'

He couldn't ascertain that Edward's grief was genuine, but he noticed that the kidnapping had changed me so much?

'Watson is aware of it too. The Afghan War did much the same to him, you know, though your vices are different, I daresay.'

It was coming. The knot in my stomach grew larger by tenfold, and I felt suddenly nauseous.

'However,' Holmes continued, 'though Watson is aware of your melancholy, he is not aware of certain *other* things.'

Somehow, through the nausea and the loud throbbing within my head, I managed to offer a weak reply. 'What?'

'Not the least of which has been made clear to me this very morning.' He nodded in the direction of my arms.

I looked down in dread to see that the sleeves of the dress I had chosen in groggy haste were not long enough to cover the entirety of my skin. Several half-healed scratches, exactly perpendicular to one another, were plainly visible, scabbed and slightly swollen red. I gasped, trying to find some way to tuck them against my body, but Holmes reached out, quick as lightning, and took hold of one of my arms.

'I confess that I am not skilled in the art of forming such words as these,' he said hurriedly, seeming embarrassed, 'but I feel that I must tell you that your suffering is not solitary. Your instinct to hide yourself away is not protective, but harmful in many ways. It is often not seen until it is too late to turn back, so pray consider that.'

He eased himself back again, leaving me shaking.

I was close to tears, my mouth slightly open in shock.

'John doesn't know you're saying this, does he?'

'No. I only observed these marks this morning.'

'Does he suspect?'

'I do not think so, no.'

'Are you going to tell him?'

'I think it would be best for him to know. He is your half-brother, the closest thing you currently have to family. It does not take someone with my powers of deduction to know that he cares deeply for you.'

Of course he cared. John was Holmes' polar opposite, though they were similar in many ways. This dual similarity and difference, though occasionally resulting in clashes, generally made them able to live and work alongside each other like twin gears, fashioned separately but meant for the same machine. My brother was all the Great Detective's rough edges, padded by all the Watson empathy that I also possessed. If Holmes cared, John was bound to care tenfold.

But that wasn't the whole of it. Of course my brother cared. Of course he'd understand. But telling him was still akin to jumping off a cliff, trusting that he'd be waiting below, stalwart as ever, to mend my broken pieces on the ground. It was overwhelming. Especially when Holmes had just startled me off the edge, then pulled me back up.

'Holmes?'

His gaze had never left me, and only the expression in his eyes changed, giving me the signal to go on.

'At least… let me be the one to tell him,' I requested.

Holmes nodded slowly. 'I can grant you that right. Now I would suggest that we consider the time. Surely the others will be waking up by now, and we will be able to inquire with Miss Camberwell and Mr Jamison as to the addresses of the late Simon Camberwell's friends.'

That was as good a dismissal as any.

We stood. As we walked towards the staircase, we met Nicole on her way down.

'You two are certainly eager to start the day,' she observed by way of greeting.

'Yes, I requested Emily's presence in the drawing room to fill me in on the events of last night's advances in the investigation.'

'There was actually something connected to that subject that Holmes was wanting to ask you.'

'What is it, Mr Holmes?' asked Nicole, adjusting her posture.

'I was interested to know, Miss Camberwell, if you had records of the addresses of your brother's friends.'

She shook her head in the negative. 'No, I'm afraid I do not. Edward was the only one of them that I ever corresponded with. The others I barely knew, and only saw a few times. They were around during holidays and, of course, the visit of a few months ago. I assume that you still wish to speak with them for the investigation?'

'That is correct.'

'Well, in that case, I'm sure that Edward will be able to help you. I am very sorry that I can't be of assistance.'

Of course, we could have just searched Simon's room, and Holmes would surely have thought of it, but it seemed he wanted the information from Edward instead. All the better to gauge whatever it was that the detective gauged from seemingly innocuous encounters.

It was good to have him acting himself again, even if it meant he saw right through me.

We were soon joined on the ground floor by John, Andrew, and Lestrade.

Holmes gave me a covert look, and I stared at the floor. It wasn't at all that after what Holmes had said I was having any qualms about telling my brother; it was just that I wasn't ready. The entire possibility hadn't been sprung on me until today, and it certainly hadn't been expected. I needed at least a couple of days to consider how to approach the subject. How to alert him that I was jumping off a cliff. How to tell him to be ready to catch me.

Nicole looked around at our small group, evidently noticing, as was plain, that Edward was not among us.

'Well,' she said, 'if we all adjourn to the dining room, I will ring for breakfast. I am sure that Edward will join us shortly.'

No doubt he had merely overslept, as I knew I would have done myself had Holmes not roused me so early. Given this probability, there were no murmurs of disagreement as we all started in the direction of the dining room.

Breakfast was finished, and a slightly uneasy feeling was starting to spread throughout the room, for Edward had not joined our diminished party.

'Does anyone object to my going to rouse him?' asked Andrew, preparing to stand.

No one spoke up, so he took that as an affirmative and left.

The silence he left in his wake was heavy, stretching to eternity. In reality, the clock only ticked out a minute and a half before Andrew's hurried footsteps sliced the stifling quiet.

'Andrew?' My voice was apprehensive. He was gasping for air like a drowning man.

'Edward Jamison is dead.'

Chapter 12: Murder Most Foul

Murder most foul, as in the best it is,
But this most foul, strange, and unnatural.
– William Shakespeare

Someone's fork clattered on the table. I turned to see Nicole's face had gone a sort of ashen grey.

'How?' John inquired darkly.

'Don't be absurd, Watson, we know how he died,' Holmes admonished. 'The question is how was the poison administered? Did he have a drink taken to him?'

'That's what I meant, Holmes...' John's counter went mostly unnoticed.

Andrew shook his head. 'I didn't see anything like that. I didn't look any closer. I know time is of the essence.'

Holmes, John, and Lestrade stood. I started to as well, but John held up a hand.

'Emily, stay here with Miss Camberwell.'

Andrew moved to leave the room again, but quick as lightning, John stopped him too. 'No, Mr Lynch, stay with the girls.'

Andrew opened his mouth to protest. 'But I—'

'Unless you supervise them, there is no telling where they'll run off to.'

'Yes, Doctor.'

John nodded briskly and followed Holmes and Lestrade. We sat in silence for several moments before I became aware that Nicole was hyperventilating, albeit softly. I turned towards her and put a hand on her arm.

At my motion, Andrew looked up sharply. He appeared to have been engaged in studying the fringe on the tablecloth.

'Are you all right, Nicole?'

Unable to say anything, she quickly shook her head.

'Do you need fresh air?' I asked.

She nodded.

'Absolutely not,' Andrew cut in. 'Doctor Watson will murder me if they come back and we're not here. Edward's body is still warm. The killer could still be close by.'

'Don't be ridiculous, the poison takes hours to kill, the murderer could have come in the night.'

'And do you realise how secluded this town is? He couldn't have gone far.'

'Andrew, please. Just to the front steps, and only for a few moments, until she can catch her breath.'

He looked away but shook his head again.

'Would you rather she faint?'

'Fine! But only for a moment. Here, help me hold her up.'

We helped Nicole stand, supporting her trembling figure until we were outside. The cold morning breeze blew against my face. I could see that Nicole was already improving. She was leaning against one of the tall pillars, eyes closed, letting the wind blow loose strands of hair around her face.

A moment later, she opened her eyes and looked at us. 'I need to clear my head.'

'You are clearing your head,' replied Andrew tersely.

'Andrew, good Lord! You are taking this far too seriously!' I exclaimed.

'Emily, there is a dead body upstairs, the third in a week! The man was murdered not even half an hour ago!'

As if she hadn't heard any of this, Nicole said in the same soft voice, 'I think I need to take a walk.'

Andrew gave me an alarmed look, and I returned it. The girl was in shock, undoubtedly.

'We should go back inside, Nicole,' Andrew said warily, approaching her slowly in case she needed support.

She locked her gaze on him. I confess that I was surprised, for her eyes were determined, without a hint of the vague, glazed look of a person in shock.

'Please. I need to go for a walk. Just a short one. You can come with me.'

Andrew gave a quick glance at the door.

'It's all right,' I said to him. 'She seems to be in no danger at present.'

'Can you walk on your own?' Andrew asked.

'I am fine.'

Nicole took a deep breath before straightening. She was steady, like an old, weathered oak that is never blown down, although it may be slightly bent and rocked with each storm. She began walking down the steps at a brisk pace, and we had no choice but to follow, Andrew's hand slipping into mine as we feverishly attempted to keep up. Our gait bordered on sprinting.

Nicole quickly made her way through the woods. She had the obvious advantage over us, as she knew every dip and rise in the landscape surrounding Rosedale Abbey, the location of every tree root and every stone that protruded the surface of the soil. After a while, she took a turn, curving through the trees in an unfamiliar direction. A musty, damp scent was wafting through the air, and I got a sinking feeling in my stomach.

'Nicole, where are we going?' I asked, struggling for breath.

She did not reply, nor did she need to, for it became painstakingly obvious within a few seconds. There was a large, gaping hole in the side of a hill, the border of it framed with wood so that it would not cave in. A stream of cold air flowed eerily out of it, like some kind of mouth engaged in an eternal act of gasping. Chunks of rock and abandoned broken pieces of pickaxes were scattered around. There was a sort of miniature train track that ran into the darkness of the hillside, forming what looked like a tongue for the sinister mouth. There could be no doubt that this was the entrance to the mines. One of them, anyway.

Andrew stared in awe. Shaking himself out of his stupor quickly, he grabbed Nicole's arm. 'What are we doing here?'

'It's all right,' she said. 'This is only one of the smaller entrances. It's an older one, as well. It isn't even used anymore.'

'How far are we from the house?' I asked.

'Not too far,' she said with a glance behind us.

'You didn't answer me, Nicole,' said Andrew, shivering as a cold gust of wind blew. 'What are we doing here?'

'The motive for these murders is someone wanting the mines closed... I had to come and see.'

'Come see what? There's nothing here. It's an abandoned mine entrance, Nicole, that's it.'

'Andrew, she's right. It can't hurt to look around.'

Although an ominous intuition was brewing within me, I couldn't pass up the possibility of something, *anything,* that might help our case, as long as we were here.

But our conversation was interrupted by a noise from within the mines. It was the sound of rocks scrabbling and wood creaking. As if someone, or something, was crawling inside.

'Let's go,' Andrew said rigidly. 'We shouldn't be here, especially not now.'

But I was already moving closer to the entrance. Curiosity was pulling me forward, and no amount of reason could stop me.

I turned to Nicole. 'Have you been here before?'

She nodded, seeming frozen in place. 'Yes, a great number of times.'

'Are there any lights lying about?'

She promptly strode to a large rock and reached behind it, pulling out an old oil lantern and conjuring a match seemingly out of thin air.

'The miners always kept an emergency matchbook adhered with wax to the bottom of the lantern,' she explained, striking the match before Andrew could move to stop her.

'No,' he said, pointing a finger in our direction. 'Neither of you are going to enter that mineshaft. We are going to put that lantern out and go back the way we came. When we reach the house, we will report to Holmes that we heard something at the mine entrance. I imagine we will be chastised, especially me.'

'Andrew, aren't you just a little curious to know what made that noise?' I asked.

'I'm sure it was some animal.'

Nicole scoffed. 'No, you're not. You're too scared.'

'I am not scared! I am showing reason!'

'Good investigation calls for more risks than reason,' I said, taking the lantern from Nicole and holding it out. 'You can either stay here or take this lantern and lead the way.'

Andrew tightened his lips and gave me a look, but after a moment of silent heated debate passing between us, he angrily snatched the light from my hand.

'At the first sign of further trouble, we turn back.' He stalked contemptuously into the mouth of the hollowed-out hillside.

Nicole and I followed behind. As the cold air hit us, she grabbed my arm tightly. I winced as she hit one of my scratches, but resisted the urge to jerk away. I only bit my lip softly and reached for Andrew with my other hand for some reassurance. He put out his free hand behind him, all of us walking together carefully along the tracks in a closely knit clump.

The area that was illuminated by our meagre light source was a long corridor of stone, with the track for what must have been mine carts running down the centre. The walkway was closed by stone only on one side. On the other side was a rather unsteady looking wooden railing, the supports of which were all but eaten away by some sort of fungus.

I peered over the railing and saw a gigantic, ragged pit which descended into darkness. The stone-paved edge around the precipice went all the way around the cave-like space, and several other corridors seemed to branch out from here on the other side. Moisture dripped from the ceiling above, pooling in a slight depression in the ground.

Footsteps came from somewhere behind us, the resounding echo dispersing them through the cavernous space.

We all stopped short. Andrew held the lantern aloft, hoping that it would show some part of whoever was in here with us.

His light illuminated a faint silhouette, which soon disappeared from view.

'Did they leave?' Nicole asked breathlessly.

'I think they— *Run!*'

'What?' I gasped in confusion.

'Run,' Andrew shouted again, pulling us further into the mine.

Nicole and I glanced at one another, perplexed, but we turned and ran anyway. Andrew was two steps behind us, ushering us on. I was glad in a moment for his warning, for there was a sudden flash of light and smoke, and a loud, thundering boom, the force of which sent us flying into the stone wall. We landed in a coughing heap, waving dust away from our eyes as the debris cleared.

The lantern had gone out, leaving us in pitch dark. Andrew fumbled for a match to relight it. He held it up and cursed.

'There's no light from outside anymore.'

We scrambled to our feet. He began making his way through a sea of fallen rocks that now lay between us and the entrance. Nicole and I followed close behind, slightly slower because of our long skirts, still coughing violently. As we got closer to where we had come in, it became quite apparent that the entrance was now blocked.

We were trapped.

Chapter 13: In Wand'ring Mazes Lost

Others apart sat on a hill retir'd,
In thoughts more elevate, and reason'd high
Of Providence, foreknowledge, will, and fate,
Fix'd fate, free will, foreknowledge absolute,
And found no end, in wand'ring mazes lost.
— John Milton

For the next few hours we navigated the labyrinthine corridors, holding our breath as much as we could, for as we made our way deeper into the mine, the dank, metallic smell of rock turned acrid – a sign that we were growing nearer to the current site of excavation.

More than a few times, we walked around in large circles without realising it. The consensus was that if we followed our noses stronger, we would eventually reach another entrance.

I was walking shoulder to shoulder with Andrew, gripping him by the elbow and trying not to think about the puddle I'd just stepped in, when I heard a tentative voice behind us.

'I think you two should come look at this.'

We both stopped in our tracks and turned to see Nicole, standing in front of the entrance to an offshoot of the passageway, wringing her hands in front of her.

Andrew and I stepped gingerly over a shallow crater to see what she had found. She lifted a finger and pointed into the dark, shadowy alley. I squinted, only being able to make out a dark mass until Andrew lifted the lantern.

A body lay crumpled in the passage.

Andrew cursed and shoved the lantern into my hands, going to kneel by the corpse. I didn't have to watch him turn it over to be certain that it wasn't a mine worker. The clothes were not shabby, and the only reason that they could appear to be at first glance was that the body was covered head to toe in dirt and dust. The limp figure wore a black overcoat. From what I could see in the dim light of our lantern, the nails were perfectly clean and manicured.

Andrew grunted, pushing at the deceased's shoulder until it gave way, rolling flat onto its back, head lolling to the side like a ragdoll.

Nicole let out a small gasp and jumped back a few inches.

'You know him?' Andrew raised his eyebrows.

She nodded rapidly. 'That's Leslie.'

I looked from Andrew, to the body, to Nicole. 'As in your brother's friend Leslie?'

'Yes. Is he—' I knew that she had been about to say *dead*, but had cut herself off.

Andrew nodded solemnly. 'I'm afraid so. He's still slightly warm.'

Nicole closed her eyes, wrapping her arms around herself. 'Was it poison?'

Andrew furrowed his brow and looked down at the body. I knelt to look as well. The overcoat was buttoned, but there was something crusted on it.

'Andrew, look at that,' I pointed.

He nodded and deftly began undoing the buttons. When it was done, he tried to pull the coat away from the body, but it stuck. He grunted and yanked harder. A part of the shirt tore off with it, revealing a gaping hole in the chest cavity. It had stopped oozing blood, but it still seemed fresh.

'...No,' Andrew said after a moment of looking at the wound in puzzlement. 'He was stabbed.'

Nicole opened her eyes. *'What?'*

I leaned back on my heels and considered for a moment how fortunate we were that the smell of the ores was so strong, for it covered up that musk of death. Then again, if Nicole hadn't spotted it, we likely would never have found it at all.

'Why was he stabbed and not poisoned?' I asked. 'And why was he even here at all?'

'I don't think he was,' Andrew said, shaking his head. 'He wouldn't have collapsed in that position. He was moved from somewhere else.'

'No, it was here,' Nicole said, the tone of her voice vague as her gaze locked on something on the wall a few feet away. 'Close to here, anyway. Bring the light over.'

Andrew scrambled to his feet, offering a hand to me. We both took a few steps to see what Nicole was referring to.

Blood. Smears of it along the stone wall. I remembered seeing it out of the corner of my eye a few minutes ago when we were passing by, but I had assumed it was only rust.

'That means he was stabbed back here somewhere,' I murmured, walking back the way we had come slowly, a vision suddenly springing to my mind.

116

A man with a fatal wound in his chest, struggling, staggering, trying desperately to find his way out, to get help. He clutches at his injury, bleeding all over his own hands. His hands go to the rock wall for support as he inches along, every breath agonising as he fights the urge to collapse. At the ingress of the offshoot, the wall ends for a space of about four feet, and he cannot stand for that distance on his own. He falls onto the ground just inside the smaller passageway with a cry, and his breathing becomes increasingly ragged and feeble until it stops altogether.

'Maybe he wasn't dragged or moved at all...'

'What?' Andrew sprinted up behind me, Nicole close behind him. 'What are you talking about?'

'The blood on the wall, Andrew. He was stabbed back here somewhere and dragged himself. He was trying to escape.'

'From whom?' Nicole's voice shook with fear.

I stopped in my tracks.

Oh my God.

'Andrew, you said he was still slightly warm, right?'

'Yes.'

'So, he's been dead for a few hours.'

'Right...'

'How long have we been here?'

'At least... *oh my God.*' Andrew echoed my own thoughts.

'What am I missing?' Nicole asked in a small voice.

I turned to her. 'We've been stuck in here for at least a few hours, Nicole. Someone was in here with us and they shut us in. What we heard from outside? That was Leslie dragging himself, and the killer watching, afraid we were too close. Afraid we'd find him before he died.'

She inhaled sharply, her eyes wide with alarm. 'So that person wasn't merely skulking in the shadows watching us.'

117

I backed up a few steps and leaned against the opposite wall, letting out a breath slowly. I winced as the putrid air filled my nose and lungs.

'These connections are all very well and good, but that still doesn't explain what Leslie was doing here in the first place. And not just here in the mines, but *here.* Why was he in the area?'

I glanced at Nicole, hoping that she would be able to offer some explanation. Perhaps she had sent telegrams to friends other than Edward.

'I didn't contact him, or any of the others. Only Edward. He was the closest to us, and I was afraid. The others never even crossed my mind.'

'Is there any other way he could have heard about Simon's death?' Andrew asked.

'Perhaps Edward sent him a telegram?'

'We can infer all we want, but it's a little too late to ask either of them.' I gestured with an arm at the body. 'And besides, if he was here because of Simon's death, why would he not have come to the estate first?'

'Maybe he realised the mines were connected to the murders and came here looking for some clue?' Andrew mused, leaning against the wall by the ingress and less than ceremoniously removing himself when he realised he was leaning directly on top of a smear of blood.

'Perhaps we could start by finding out if that's why he was here,' Nicole suggested. 'If Edward wrote to him, maybe he has – had – some physical confirmation of that. We should return anyway, and alert them that there's another body.'

'Damn it, we're in hot water,' Andrew groaned. 'We've been gone for *hours*. I'm sure they think we've been kidnapped – or worse. We should keep going, and quickly.'

He took the lantern back from me and we started off down the main passage again. The cold breeze was getting stronger, and so was the smell. I shivered and resisted the innate urge to inhale as much as possible as we trudged onwards.

About ten minutes later, we all breathed a prayer of thanks, for we had reached another entrance. The afternoon light filtered in like a beacon. Andrew reached down and extinguished the lantern, setting it on a rock just inside the mine.

The daylight felt like a gift after hours in the dim, despite the initial discomfort it brought us.

'All right, Nicole, how far is it back to the house?' Andrew asked, turning his head this way and that.

We were close to the woods; there was only about fifty yards between the gaping hillside and the influx of trees. However, they extended as far as could be seen, and I had no idea how Nicole could be certain of our whereabouts. She shielded her eyes with her hand, stood on her tiptoes, and peered around.

'The path is over there,' she pointed a small distance to the left. 'We can follow it straight back to the house.'

Andrew nodded and grabbed me with one hand, Nicole with the other. Soon, the path came into focus and we began half sprinting, slowing to a walk again as Rosedale Abbey came into view.

'You had better both be prepared for the reprimand we are going to receive,' Andrew muttered, a hint of contempt still in his voice now that the adrenaline had passed.

I gave him a look. 'Andrew, we have an excuse!'

He sighed exasperatedly. 'An excuse for being gone so long? Yes. An excuse for leaving in the first place? Not so much. I was supposed to keep you at the table. And not even for that long! As far as my responsibilities go, I have been a complete failure.'

We were finally drawing nearer to the house. I squinted as we crossed the spacious lawn, looking for a sign of movement from anyone watching for us to come back.

At first, I saw nothing. Then, as we drew close, a curtain closed with a slight flourish. A moment later, the door swung open and Lestrade came dashing down the front steps towards us.

'Where in the *hell* have you been?'

'We can explain, Inspector,' Nicole jumped in hurriedly.

Andrew scoffed semi-hysterically. 'Yes, *you'd* better explain. You're the one who wanted to leave in the first place!'

Nicole turned on him. '*You're* the one who let me!'

Lestrade held up a hand. 'Save it, all of you. Holmes and the Doctor are searching the woods on the other side of the house looking for you. I will fetch them. Stay here.'

He started to walk off, but then evidently reconsidered his instructions and turned back to us, pointing. 'Actually, no. Come with me.'

His manner was harsh, and as he led us behind the house and towards the woods, I thought about how I had not before seen him look so angry and disappointed.

I tried not to look at the row of solemn gravestones out of the corner of my eye, the dirt under two of them still fresh. As we continued walking, Andrew shot Nicole and I an angry glare. Before I could fully register what was happening, they had both stopped walking.

'Stop looking at me as though this is entirely my fault!' Nicole spat. 'You could have stopped me from leaving if you had wanted. But you didn't! This is more your fault than anything!'

'*My* fault?' Andrew let out a barking laugh. 'You were the one with not enough common sense to follow instructions in the first place!'

With fury in her eyes, Nicole reached out and gave Andrew a hard shove. He stumbled backward, then tried to lash back at her.

Alarmed, I stepped between them.

'Both of you, stop,' I said firmly, reaching out both of my arms to catch Andrew before he could make any attempt to hurt Nicole.

'*You're* telling *me* to stop?' He goaded incredulously. 'You, little miss *"it can't hurt to go in and look around, nothing will happen"*?'

Why were they both being so unreasonable?

Then it dawned on me.

The lead.

The acrid, toxic fumes, wending their way into brains, twisting the imagination, turning molehills into mountains and pitting people against each other.

But why was it affecting them and not me? Holmes had fallen prey to it after walking at the mines – and we had spent hours there. Had they somehow spent more time near the mines than I? Come to think of it, why was Andrew already up when Nicole left her room last night? What were they doing? Was Andrew with her? Had they taken a stroll by the mines, alone, then come back and tried to play off their being awake as Nicole's anxieties? Had they been—

Wait, no.

That was how the lead worked.

That was precisely how every clash in town Nicole had mentioned started. How Edward had become convinced Simon was stealing his profits. A walk by the mines on the way into town, discussing the deal they'd made, more than a little alcohol added to their blood…

A delectable recipe for conflict. A perfect setup for death.

It wasn't at all that I wasn't being affected. The toxins in the air preyed upon human paranoia, making each one think that they were the only one not affected.

Making us all believe everyone was conspiring against us.

Making us believe there was a monster deep in the Earth. There was, I suppose, but the monster was the very thing being sought. The monster was nature itself.

I shuddered. We all needed a dose of whatever antidote John had given to Holmes.

The world came back into focus around me, and I realised that I was still holding Andrew's arms, my grip growing tighter. He had made no move to pull himself away, and I let go before I did any damage.

I began to walk, waving them both onwards, trying to conceal my shaking limbs. We sprinted to catch up to Lestrade, who had stopped at the edge of the wood to watch the spat.

We went on into the trees until at last we heard voices and leaves crunching underfoot. They stopped speaking abruptly as we approached.

'Lestrade, is that you?' Holmes called out.

'Yes, Holmes, it's me. I have them. They came back to the house.'

I heard a cry of triumph from Holmes and a loud sigh of relief from my brother, and the two of them lumbered into view.

'Where the devil have you been?' John asked, rushing over and inspecting us for injuries. 'Your arms are scratched to bits and – Andrew, *why* is there blood on your back?'

Andrew made a face of slight disgust and immediately shrugged off his vest.

'I will explain, John,' I said, stepping in for all of us, for Nicole was still filled with lead-induced fury and Andrew was busy examining his vest with distaste.

'And it had better be a damn good explanation,' Holmes said, looking us up and down with a critical eye. 'Why were you in the mines?'

Lestrade looked sharply at Holmes. 'What? How do you know that's where they were?'

Holmes gestured at us exasperatedly, giving Lestrade the same sort of look you give a small child who is asking trivial and needless questions.

'*Look at them, Lestrade.* They're all dusty! Where else would they have gotten themselves so covered in dust?'

I sighed. 'Nicole wanted to go for a short walk to clear her head, so we followed. We ended up at one of the smaller, unused mine entrances. She wanted to look around, and we decided it couldn't hurt.'

'*We* decided? *You* decided that all on your own, Emily,' Andrew cut in. 'If it were up to me, we would have come straight back.'

'*Andrew!*' I admonished, holding up a hand to silence him. 'We heard a sound like someone was inside, so we lit a lantern and went in to see if anyone was there. Before we could see who it was, they had lit a stick of dynamite and vanished. The explosion triggered a rockslide and blocked the entrance, so we had to find another way out. I admit that we got lost in the passages more than once. That's what took us so long.'

Before I could explain about the body, John held up a hand, thinking I was finished.

'First of all, Andrew, it was irresponsible of you to let Nicole and Emily leave the house in the first place. Secondly, Nicole, what exactly possessed you to go wandering about down there? And third, Emily, it was just as irresponsible to go along with any of it. You have been living with Holmes and I for a couple of months now, so surely you have learned some kind of common sense within that time.'

I looked at the ground sheepishly for a moment before raising my head. 'But there's something else. When we were in there, we found another body. It was Leslie, another of Simon's friends.'

123

All three drew back slightly at my words, though Holmes was less violently surprised. The detective, as a logical thinker, didn't allow himself to be taken aback by any course of events, having organised and theorised all possible progressions like the moves in a game of chess within his head. But despite all this, I could still tell that he had been caught off guard by my news.

'How fresh is the body?' he asked, his eyes glinting metallically, the signal that somewhere behind them, gears were grinding fiercely inside the great mind.

'We found him only a little while ago,' Andrew chimed in. 'Thirty minutes, at most. At that time, I would say he had been dead for about three or four hours.'

Holmes raised his eyebrows. 'And are you qualified to estimate that, Mr Lynch?'

Although he was still listening, rapt, to every detail we gave, he still beheld a note of the scepticism that I knew he held towards Andrew and his privileges as son of the Chief Commissioner of the Metropolitan Police.

Andrew's lips tightened almost imperceptibly. I almost told Holmes that this was not a good time to question Andrew's ability to be certain. Fortunately, however, he seemed to have regained the virtue of passivity for the present.

'Not officially, no, but I have been around enough of those who are to pick up some quality indications. Based on the surrounding temperature in relation to that of the body, it had stopped giving off heat between three and four hours ago.'

'Poisoned?' John asked.

Andrew shook his head. 'No. Stabbed. Emily thinks he tried to find his way out and dragged himself along the wall for some time before collapsing. We found him in the entrance to a smaller offshoot of the main tunnel. Prior to that, there were smears of blood along the wall from him trying to support himself. That's why there's blood on the back of my vest. I accidentally leaned against it.'

'Significant blood loss causes the body to cool more rapidly,' John explained. 'It may not have been quite as long ago as you think.'

'But what was this Leslie doing in the mines in the first place?' Lestrade asked.

'We're not sure,' Nicole said, speaking at last, her sudden rage seeming to have melted away. 'We thought perhaps Edward had contacted him after receiving my telegram about Simon's death. After we'd made it back, we wanted to look in his things and see if he had some confirmation of that, perhaps a draft of the document or a reply of some sort.'

'We are fairly sure, though,' I added, 'that whatever he was doing there was the reason he was killed. Maybe he realised that the mines were the reason for the murders and went looking for answers. Maybe he found them. Either way, it warranted a quick death. There wasn't enough time to poison him.'

Holmes nodded in agreement. 'Very true, Emily. Now, you three take us back there so we can have a look.'

'I'll lead the way.' Nicole nodded tersely and led us back to the front of the house and down the path again.

Before we made it too far, I stopped in front and held up my hands to stop our progress.

'After we left the mines, Andrew and Nicole had an argument, and I found myself thinking irrationally as well. It seems pointless to do it now, seeing as we are heading back to the source, but once we return to the house, I suggest we all take a dose of the antidote John gave Holmes last night.'

My brother nodded in agreement. 'That would be a prudent decision. We cannot afford to be out of our heads.'

As we continued walking, I felt Holmes' eyes on me and slowed my pace to be even with him.

'Have you told Andrew?' he asked quietly.

I had been watching the ground in front of me carefully, taking caution not to stumble on any rocks or tree roots, but at this I sharply raised my head and looked at Holmes in surprise.

'Andrew? Why?'

'Emily, despite any doubts I might have regarding the sincerity and depth of his knowledge in the field of criminal investigation, I know that he has grown to care for you just as much as Watson, if not entirely in the same way. I would risk my reputation to say that he would be very upset if he found out later rather than sooner.'

I bit my lip, realising that he was entirely right. I had been too caught up in hiding my secret to consider that those I was shutting out cared for me too much to condone my hiding it. And even if they didn't catch on very quickly, it was inevitable that they eventually would, just as Holmes had. I had to admit that it was by far preferable that they hear it from me than find out on their own, even if the latter was the easier road.

At that moment I considered asking Holmes if he had ever done the same thing. His words about understanding what I was feeling this morning had been very oddly placed had he not truly been able to empathise. But I was not bold enough to formulate a coherent sounding sentence on the subject, and the foul odour of the mines was creeping very close, so I stayed silent.

Seeing that the main entrance to the mine was within sight, Holmes dashed ahead, stopping at the ingress.

'Approximately how far is the body?' he asked, looking between the three of us.

'About ten minutes of a walk,' I replied.

Nicole walked over to the large rock and picked up the lantern we had left, striking a third match to light it.

Holmes nodded. 'Nicole, I trust you remember enough to lead the way?'

She nodded and raised the lantern up to provide a sustainable light source. Letting out a steadying breath, she walked into the mouth of the hillside, all of us following close behind.

Andrew looked over at me and moved closer, slipping his hand into mine. My breath caught in my throat as he did so and Holmes' words came floating back to me, my arm burning in response. I knew that the detective had been right. I needed to tell him. For Heaven's sake, we were fully romantic, he was bound to notice at some point.

In fact, I was quite surprised that he hadn't already, as he had spent the last month instructing me in various forms of self-defence. But now was most certainly not the right time. I needed time to think over what I needed to say.

I was broken out of my thoughts by the entire group coming to a sudden halt. Nicole had her free hand in front of her face.

'I don't understand,' she stammered out. 'How—'

'Perhaps you were mistaken about there being a body,' Lestrade said dryly.

'We were not mistaken,' Andrew retorted. 'I turned it over myself.'

I furrowed my brow, moving over a little bit to be able to see. My hand flew to my mouth.

The body was gone.

Chapter 14: An Untimely Grave

Thou shalt confess the vain pursuit of human glory yields no fruit but an untimely grave.
– Thomas Carew

Absolutely impossible.

John's arms were crossed, a disgruntled look on his face.

'I think Lestrade is right,' he said sceptically, his moustache bristling slightly with annoyance. 'I don't see a body here, nor any evidence that there was one. I'm sure lead isn't the only ore in this place. If a vein of mercury was unintentionally exposed, it would cause vivid hallucinations.'

Andrew's hand had left mine, now slack at his side. Nicole numbly walked over and came to a halt at my other side. The three of us looked at one another, completely speechless.

'Don't be ridiculous, of course there was a body here!' Holmes exclaimed, snatching the lantern and holding it up close to the wall. 'Look here! Smears of blood, just as they said.'

'That looks like rust to me, Holmes,' Lestrade said, squinting slightly.

Andrew stiffened and pointed a finger at Lestrade. 'I did not have *rust* on the back of my vest!'

Holmes wiped a finger across the substance and sniffed it, looking as though he wanted to say something, but didn't have a fully formulated thought. He waved the lantern around the space a bit, and leapt back in the passage a few feet, squatting close to the ground to illuminate a puddle.

We stepped closer to see. I gasped again, for the small pool of liquid on the ground was thick, opaque, and reddish-brown. It was on the spot where I had tread in a puddle just before we found Leslie's body. My left foot gave an involuntary twitch. No doubt my shoe and the hem of my skirt were now soaked with it.

'You were saying there was no body?' Holmes challenged.

'Where the hell do you suppose it went?' asked Lestrade.

'I would imagine that the killer took it.'

'Took it where?' I asked. 'We saw him leave, and directly afterwards we were blocked in.'

'There are other entrances,' Nicole pointed out.

Holmes nodded. 'It is more than likely that after the killer made sure you three couldn't follow him, he looped around the outside to the main entrance. There he waited until he knew you were out of his way and came back to dispose of the body.'

'But where would he have taken it? We weren't gone from here very long at all, and it's no easy thing to carry a corpse. Besides, look here at the ground. I don't see any scuff or blood marks to show that the body was dragged anywhere. He would have had to lift the deceased off the ground and carry him. Unless he's Herculean, it can't have been anywhere particularly far.'

'What about somewhere else in the mine?' John asked. 'It's not a long distance, and I'm sure there's a lot of unused branches.'

Holmes let out a laugh and clapped his hands together, causing an echo. 'Watson, that's brilliant!'

'Shall we split up?' Lestrade suggested. 'We would cover a great deal more ground that way.'

Holmes raised his eyebrows.

'I doubt splitting up would do us much good, Lestrade,' I snorted.

'And why not?'

'We only have one lantern,' Holmes lifted it to illustrate.

Lestrade clapped his hands together, tightening his lips with the air of one who was about to claim that he had known all along.

'Together it is.'

And we set off as a group, Holmes at the front of our party, holding the lantern high to illuminate our paths.

We turned down various offshoots, peering into innumerable nooks and crannies shrouded in gloomy darkness, searching for what seemed to be hours. Even with the time we had spent wandering the mines before, I had not imagined that they could be so vast.

A few yards ahead of us, beyond the reach of the lantern's wavering circle of light, came the unmistakable, eerily heavy sound of something being dragged across the ground. The cacophony reverberated off every stone wall around us. It was impossible to determine whether it was coming from the main passage or one of the smaller offshoots.

Holmes held up a hand, but none of us needed the warning. We all abruptly halted, causing Nicole to nearly trip over Andrew's left shoe. He immediately shot out an arm to steady her. I held my breath.

'Who's there?' Holmes called out into the darkness, slowly and silently squatting to place the lantern gently on the ground.

'Holmes, what are you—' John began under his breath. But he did not have time to finish, for the answer quickly became obvious.

A gunshot echoed with a sharp crack, and Andrew pulled me sideways into him as it whizzed past Holmes' collar, barely an inch from where my head had been a split second before. I let out my breath in a small gasp.

Both hands now free, Holmes pulled his weapon out of his coat, but not before John had whipped out his revolver, simultaneously aiming over Holmes' shoulder and shifting his body in front of mine.

Lestrade drew his own gun and covered Holmes' other side, but quickly turned to us and hissed, 'You three, run. Andrew, get them back to the house immediately. Lock the doors and secure the building. Do not let anyone in until you see us come back.'

Without even a nod in reply, Andrew turned tail and pushed us forward, setting us off at a sprint towards what might or not be the exit. We didn't have any time to stop and confer about which twists and turns would lead us back to the entrance.

From behind us came the cracks of returning gunshots, and the subsequent clinks as the bullets hit the walls, chipping off pieces of stone. Our breathing eventually became laboured, my lungs seared with the effort of gasping for air, and we were forced to duck into an offshoot to stop for breath.

After a moment, more shots sounded, closer to us, and a bullet struck a piece of stone directly above my head, which crumbled and fell in a powdery dust into my hair.

No, that's impossible, I thought, for this meant that there was more than one shooter. Although I tried, I did not have a chance to look around for the source, for Andrew pulled us out from against the wall, urging us further and further ahead of him.

We all knew that there was no time to stay together. Although we were fleeing as a single group, we were each running separately, as fast as we could. And though Andrew was clearly faster than both of us, he trailed behind to act as a shield between us and the shooter.

Soon enough, I had lost all inclination of where he was, and even Nicole. I barely noticed when I passed the entrance of the mines. Trees surrounded me for some time before I realised and slowed to a halt for breath, throwing myself behind a particularly large trunk, kneeling on the ground and gasping for breath. My vision was blurry after so long blindly running through the dark; it took me a moment to adjust to the change in surroundings.

It was growing dark outside. I could not see the direction of the sunset within the dense prison of trees. I used the miniscule amount of light left to peer around me. Something was familiar about this place. My eyes darted from a strange imprint in the blanket of wet leaves on the ground, as of something laying there for a prolonged amount of time, to the few brown leaves still adorning the branches of the trees around me, to the tangle of tree roots and the rotting log on the ground.

This was the spot where we had found Simon Camberwell's body just days before.

But something was different, and not just the absence of the body. Something was… new. Wincing as my breath seared my throat and lungs once again, I inhaled deeply to clear the spots in my vision and stepped forward to peer around.

Something was embedded in the bark of a tree. I thought it was silver, but there was not yet any moonlight, so instead of a glimmer, there was only a dull, cloudy sheen. I reached forward to pull it out. As it gave way, I could see that it was a pocketknife, much like the one we had found with Simon Camberwell. In fact, as I squinted at it in the dim twilight, the style looked identical. Something was peculiar about it, though I had no idea what it was, and I snapped the knife closed and shoved it into my pocket.

A twig snapped somewhere not far from me. I started and turned around, but saw nothing. Should I wait here and see if Andrew, Nicole, or any of the others turned up? Or should I head back to the house and wait there? Or should I go looking for them?

More than one shooter was out there. Wherever I went, I was alone, with no chance of securing either the house or the woods by myself. But we had been instructed to return to the house, so heading there was far better than the others reaching the destination first and being forced to head out again in search of me or my body.

I shivered as a cold breeze rustled the scarce leaves on the trees like the decorations on a shaman's staff and headed briskly in the direction I thought led to the house.

From somewhere on my other side, I heard another twig snap. My head jerked to look. I could have sworn I saw a flurry of movement. The moment my head was turned, another shot rang out. I dove forward, hoping to avoid its trajectory.

I fell face first onto the ground. My hands and feet slid on the wet leaves as I struggled to get up. Finally, I righted myself, doing my best to dodge the whistling paths of more shots as I manoeuvred through the trees. Bullets were coming at me from both sides, and although I did not slow to allow time for a deduction, something did not make sense.

It almost seemed as if the two shooters were not aiming for me, but for each other.

Finally, the house came into sight, and I flew across the lawn. A second pair of footsteps behind me slowed as a series of clicking noises began, a gun being reloaded. To a trained shooter, this only took a matter of seconds, so I didn't stop or slow and took the steps in twos. I flung open the doors and raced down the hallway, not stopping until I reached the kitchen.

The door slammed behind me. The silence in the room was shattered by the deafening pounding of blood in my ears. My breath came hard and fast, my lungs searing painfully each time I inhaled. Strands of hair had fallen loose from their clips, clinging to my forehead. My hands shook as I wiped them on my skirt and then gripped the edge of the table for support. My legs felt unsteady. I knew I would collapse if I stood on my own. Still gripping the table, I shakily moved to lean against the wall.

I didn't even know from whom I was running. All I'd heard in the chaos were the gunshots and the ensuing footsteps behind me. They had stopped to reload their weapon on the front lawn as I ran inside.

Oh, God.

That meant they couldn't be far behind me.

What was I doing? I had no time to stop for breath.

I pushed myself upright and looked frantically for something – anything – to use as a weapon. My eyes did not fall on any of the varied knives. Instead, I landed on a large, bulbous pumpkin that was sitting on the counter, ready to be carved up into some stew or pie. It was heavy, probably weighing about fifteen or twenty pounds. In my hurry, I hefted it above my head.

My arms were beginning to shake from the strain. I was afraid that I would have to set the large vegetable back on the counter, but just then the door swung open, and a figure appeared. I could only see the back of the head, for he immediately turned to wildly search the other side of the room, a gun held loosely in his hands.

Protect yourself first, ask questions later. I mustered every ounce of survival instinct within me and brought the pumpkin down on the head as hard as I could. It must have been enough, for the unfortunate owner of the cranium immediately crashed to the ground, facedown and limp. The force of the blow had done as much damage to the pumpkin as it had to the person. The outer shell had been crushed, leaving a huge mess of seeds and a stringy, mucilaginous mass.

I stood frozen in shock for a moment, watching the substance drip out of the smashed shell I held in my hands with a sort of fascination. It was beginning to mix with and congeal in the individual's hair, giving off an effect as if they had applied far too much wax in the morning.

I was still stupefied a moment later when the doors opened again with enough force that they smashed against the shelves and tables on either side of them, knocking pots and canisters of spices to the floor. My senses were both heightened and dulled at once from the adrenaline and shock. While I was unusually aware of the noise, I merely stared rather stupidly at the gathering in the doorway for an embarrassingly long while before registering Holmes, John, and Lestrade, Nicole standing right behind them.

They appeared as stunned as I was. I could thoroughly understand why. I was standing over a facedown, unconscious body, holding the shattered remains of a pumpkin, while the innards of said pumpkin dripped down onto the body. It was then that it occurred to me that I must look like a complete imbecile to have used the large squash as a weapon in a room full of knives.

'What in the blue blazes happened?' Lestrade squawked.

'Who is that?' Holmes asked, holding one arm to his chest at a strange angle.

'I-I don't know.'

John knelt to examine the body, checking for a pulse, then carefully turning it over. I had turned to set the pumpkin down on the counter behind me and froze when I turned back to see all three men plus Nicole staring at me expectantly. My gaze dropped to the limp figure on the floor. My hand flew to cover my mouth.

It was Andrew.

'Oh my God,' I breathed.

'It doesn't seem particularly dangerous,' John reassured me. 'He won't be unconscious for long, and the concussion will only be minor.'

However, his reassurances did nothing to assuage my guilt. I hadn't just hit Andrew on the head with a pumpkin. I'd *concussed* him with it.

Chapter 15: These Things Hid

Wherefore are these things hid?
– William Shakespeare

'Where in the hell is Nicole?' asked Andrew a few moments later, his words slightly slurred as he struggled back to consciousness on the drawing room sofa.

'Well, it's nice to know who you're worried about,' I commented wryly, standing behind him and plucking strings of pumpkin innards out of his hair.

He looked up at me and narrowed his eyes, trying to lean away. 'And *what* are you doing?'

I opened my mouth, attempting to form a reply, but only a small sigh came out. I closed my mouth again in exasperation and sank down onto the arm of the sofa.

'Andrew, how's your head?' John asked, returning to the room with a pitcher of water and six glasses, no doubt to distribute the antidote for the lead.

'It hurts like hell. Why does it hurt like hell? And where is Nicole?'

John handed Andrew the water and gave me a pointed look.

I sighed and plucked another pumpkin seed out of Andrew's hair as he flinched away from me, sloshing his water considerably.

'I thought you had a gun and were trying to kill me, so when you came in, I hit you over the head with a pumpkin.'

'But... the last thing I remember doing is coming into the kitchen. I was trying to find you.'

'Yes, and when you got there, I mistakenly hit you over the head with a pumpkin,' I repeated exasperatedly.

'Emily, the kitchen is full of knives!'

'I realise that now! Aren't you glad I didn't stab you?'

John stepped in between our heated debate, forcing me to step back a few paces and pointing sternly at the tray of water. I gulped one down as he tilted Andrew's head forward to inspect the large bruise that was no doubt quickly sprouting.

'Nicole is with Holmes and Lestrade upstairs. They went to search and secure the rest of the house. You have sustained a slight concussion, but it doesn't appear to be serious. There will, however, be quite a bit of bruising.'

Andrew winced as John's fingers found the spot of the impact, but he turned his head to look at me and pulled himself upright all the same.

'So first you get me shot and now you concuss me?'

'Andrew, I did not get you shot!'

'Then what was it that happened?'

'You got yourself shot!'

139

'I was rescuing you! You got kidnapped, remember?'

'You weren't supposed to be rescuing me! You were supposed to stay behind!'

'Stop it, both of you,' said John in a monotone. 'This was an accident. You're on edge; we all are. Andrew, finish that drink.'

'I'm sorry,' I said, dropping my gaze to the floor. I wasn't sure if I was speaking more to John, Andrew or myself.

'Emily, why don't you go find the others upstairs. See if they require any assistance. And take that water to them.'

I nodded in response, though John's back was turned, and I gave a last apologetic look at Andrew before turning and leaving.

My adrenaline had not yet worn off, and as I briskly climbed the stairs to the first floor, I struggled to remember exactly what had happened. We had lost each other while running from the gunshots, then I was in the woods. There was more than one shooter, and they were shooting at each other... Or was it at me? Then one of them chased me up the front lawn and I escaped inside while they were reloading their gun. And then Andrew reappeared, apparently looking for me, only I didn't realise and knocked him unconscious with a large squash.

Then that must mean he passed the shooter on the lawn. Unless he was that shooter? But then why would he have been aiming at me? Was he shooting at the second person? But where did he get the gun?

My head hurt, a combination of the confusion, my adrenaline, and the remaining effects of the lead. I reached the first-floor landing and paused, looking to my left and right for any sign of the others. A little further down the corridor, a door was ajar. Cautiously, I proceeded towards it. I pushed it open slowly with my foot, tensing my upper body to drop the tray and fight if someone was hiding in the room.

But nothing jumped out at me, or stirred at all, as the door swung open. A small suitcase lay at the foot of the bed, the handles worn and corners scuffed from a great deal of travel. This must have been Edward's room, for the coach he had ridden into town had deposited his single, hurriedly packed bag later on the day he arrived.

My suspicions were confirmed when my gaze travelled up to the body of the young, redheaded man sprawled on the bed, one arm drooping off the edge of the mattress, just as he must have been found.

Filled with unbidden curiosity, I set the tray down on the bureau by the door and stepped closer. I doubted that much investigating had been done in the room, for we had left the house this morning not long after Andrew had proclaimed that Edward was dead. It must not have been long after that that they discovered us missing and headed into the woods to search.

Edward's other arm was thrown across his chest, his hand clutching at his neck, head tilted to one side. I glanced towards the door – Holmes would be less than pleased if he discovered me moving any part of the body – and pried the hand gently away from the throat, peering closer. There was a small hole the size of a pinprick below the base of the jawline – the site of an injection, perhaps?

I narrowed my eyes for a moment, trying to recall what I had read in John's medical books about the veins and arteries in the neck. The injection must have been administered straight into the external jugular vein, which would carry the poison much more rapidly through the bloodstream than the previous methods of administration – through a cup of tea and a mug of ale. The killer had wanted him dead in a hurry – just like Leslie. Why? Had they both known something? But if Edward had known something, wouldn't he have told us?

141

With another careful glance at the doorway, I knelt by the foot of the bed and examined the suitcase. I peered closely at the clasps, worn smooth and shiny as a brass doorknob from as much use as the rest of the case. The state of the luggage seemed strange to me. Edward's voice was educated; he had obviously been raised well and attended schools of prestigious learning. I knew he had attended Eton with Simon and their other friends; he had clearly attended a university of high repute as well. His clothes were perfectly tailored and crisp. He had surely come from money, so why was his suitcase not as polished as the rest of him?

I let out a soft curse as I realised that the suitcase required a key. With luck, what I was looking for wouldn't be there at all. We needed something that confirmed he had written to Leslie and possibly any of the others when he found out about Simon's death. Something that would have made them drop everything to arrive at the estate as soon as possible. He couldn't have written to them after he arrived – that was only last night – but if he wrote to them immediately after receiving Nicole's telegram, then maybe he had brought their replies with him.

My gaze swept over the room and alighted on the desk. It was bare on top, but there were four drawers underneath. I went over to them, trying each in turn. All of them were empty.

No, no, it couldn't be.

There had to be something here.

I took another steadying breath and concentrated my gaze once again. It wouldn't do to look about frantically; I was liable to miss things. I needed to take it piece by piece.

Just then I noticed a little corner sticking out from under the desk blotter. My breath catching in my throat, I pulled it out, running my eyes over it.

Yes, this was it.

The recipient was listed as Edward Jamison, and the sender was Leslie Godwin.

Coming at once. I trust everything is ready, read the message.

Now what on earth could that mean? And for that matter, why had Edward sent out the telegram first thing? For his correspondence to arrive, and for him to receive a reply before he left, he would have had to send it out directly after receiving Nicole's message. He'd just received word that his best friend had been murdered. Why was his first reaction to send out additional messages instead of to leave at once? What could have been more important to him than to be there for Nicole and to say his farewells to Simon?

'Looking for something?' came a voice from behind me.

I gasped and turned to see Holmes standing in the doorway. I quickly slipped the telegram back onto the desk.

'I can explain.'

'John requested that you come bring us the antidote, and you found yourself sidetracked on your way to find us.'

I pursed my lips. 'Did John tell you I was coming up?'

'No. But there's a tray of water on the bureau, and I know you a bit better than you may think.'

'I know I shouldn't have come in, especially as I imagine you haven't had time to examine the scene yourself. My curiosity got the better of me.'

Holmes' jaw tensed, as though he would like to say something, but thought better of it. Instead, hands clasped behind his back, he strode further into the room, eyeing me inquisitively.

'What did you find?'

I took a breath before speaking. 'There's a needle mark on his neck, at the site of the jugular vein. I'm guessing that's where the poison entered the body.'

Holmes nodded, showing no reaction to my news, clearly waiting for more. 'And what does this tell us about his death?'

143

'That the poison spread more rapidly through his system, taking on more concentrated effects and killing him a great deal faster. Someone wanted him dead quickly, just like Leslie. Which would lead us to believe that they knew something.'

A ghost of a smile flickered across Holmes' face, and his eyes twinkled. 'Excellent. What else is there?'

'Well, the suitcase at the end of the bed is worn. It's been used a lot over the course of many years, without being replaced. I found that curious given that it's obvious Edward comes from money. His clothes are tailored and he's well-groomed; not a single patch from what I could see. So, if he does such a great amount of travelling, we must ask why his suitcase is more scuffed than his shoes. I was looking for proof that he'd written Leslie to inform him of Simon's death, but the suitcase is locked, and I don't know where the key could be. So, I went to look in the desk. The drawers were empty, but I found this tucked underneath the desk blotter.'

I reached back to pick up the telegram again and handed it to Holmes. He looked it over with a critical eye, nodding slowly and mulling it over. He pulled out the desk chair and sat down, crossing his legs and steepling his fingers.

'I was wondering,' I continued, taking the chance that he might still be listening, 'why, when he heard the news of his closest friend's death, his first reaction was to send word to one or more of his other friends instead of coming to support Nicole first and making that a concern later. What could have been more important to him? And what on earth could have warranted that reply from Leslie?'

'What made you look for that needle mark?' Holmes asked after a moment of silence. 'That isn't something one generally notices at first glance, and it looks as if his arm is covering it.'

144

'I saw that his hand was sort of clutching at that area, so I thought I'd... move it a couple inches and take a look.'

'Emily, under no circumstance from now on do I offer any support of you moving dead bodies without supervision.'

I nodded sheepishly.

'However, I would like to say that if you look closer, you will see that the hand is not in fact grasping at the throat, but at something behind it.'

'But there's nothing behind it,' I replied, my brow furrowing in confusion. 'Just the pillow.'

'Ah, but you must certainly be aware that pillows can hide fascinating things,' he said mysteriously, wagging a finger and rising from his chair.

I drew back slightly in confusion. Holmes' eyes were sharp. He had meant something else by that, I knew it. My mind flashed to my bedroom, and the small blade from John's razor carefully hidden underneath the pillow. But... he couldn't know about that, could he? He'd just found out this morning.

Pulling myself back to the here and now, I followed Holmes to where he was now bent over the bed, reaching underneath the pillow and the lifeless head that lay on top.

'Halloa!' he exclaimed after a moment, his eyes glinting as he extracted something round and gold.

'A pocket watch?' I asked, peering closer.

'Indeed, it is. I expect Lestrade and Miss Camberwell will be back downstairs by now. Would you kindly fetch them and deliver their antidotes? The end of this little game is at hand.'

Chapter 16: Time Is a Very Shadow

Our time is a very shadow that passeth away.
– The Wisdom of Solomon 2:5

A few moments later, our entire company stood gathered in the late Edward Jamison's room, the remainder of the water glasses drained, the atmosphere less inflamed. Nicole was sneaking apprehensive glances at the ashen and lifeless body on the bed. Andrew grimaced, his hair still matted with bits of squash, supporting himself against the wall in an attempt to feign steadiness. John was eyeing him critically and trying to appear otherwise.

'Holmes, what are we all doing here?' Lestrade asked, arms crossed and looking around warily. 'There's still a shooter out there, we should be looking for him! Especially considering that one of our bullets struck him in the mines. By the way, excellent shot, Doctor.'

My brother thinned his lips and nodded. 'Best in my unit, though I don't consider warfare a point of pride.'

'Lestrade, there was more than one shooter,' I informed him, shaking my head. 'When we were running, someone else began shooting at us. In the chaos, we separated, and I was running through the woods when more shots sounded. Only they were coming at me from both sides, so there were at least two more shooters. The thing was, it didn't seem like they were aiming for me. Otherwise, with two of them there, it's more than likely I would have been hit at least once. It seemed more like they were shooting at each other, and I was only caught in the crossfire.'

Nicole's brow furrowed. 'Well, that's peculiar. Why would two shooters, who appeared to be after us, be shooting at each other?'

At this moment I happened to look over at Andrew, who was shifting rather uncomfortably, avoiding my gaze. Finally, he looked up. When his eyes connected with mine, and he broke down.

'You… you were caught in the middle of that?'

I sighed, as I suspected I was about to have my theory confirmed. 'Andrew, what did you do?'

'Outside the mines I found a gun and some clips of ammunition. Someone else must have dropped them in their haste. So, I picked them up and loaded the gun. I started into the woods and caught a glimpse of another figure, also armed. I figured they couldn't be on our side, so I started shooting at them, and they returned fire. Emily, I had no idea you were out there too, until I saw you run into the house. I greatly apologise.'

'Wait.' I held up my hand. 'Was that you reloading your gun on the lawn? I heard someone behind me, so I kept running inside, and that's when I found my way into the kitchen.'

Andrew nodded. 'I saw you running for the house, and I knew the other shooter was still behind me. I covered you in hopes that you could get away. The shooter ran off towards the town after that. I never saw his face.'

I felt an odd sort of burning sensation in my gut, and suddenly I felt rather bashful looking in Andrew's direction at the thought of what lengths he had gone to in order to protect me.

'So, there were at least *two* shooters total, possibly more,' Lestrade concluded. 'That still does nothing to tell us why we are in front of this dead man, who can no longer tell us anything of importance, rather than hunting down these perpetrators.'

Holmes groaned. 'Lestrade, you cannot possibly have just insinuated that Mr Jamison here can tell us nothing of importance. Why do you think you call *me* to the scenes of your murders? Why did you call *me* to Lauriston Gardens to view Enoch Drebber's body? Was it not because you had great reverence for my ability to interpret what the dead have to tell us?'

'All right, pray tell us what Mr Jamison has to say.'

A small smirk flitted across Holmes' face. I could tell that he was greatly enjoying the thrill that was found in this dramatic spotlight.

'Edward Jamison did not consume any beverage containing our *dose mortelle*. As Emily informed me that she observed, there is an injection below his jawline. Watson, that is the site of the external jugular, is it not?'

John nodded tersely in response to the question, his gaze fixed and stance rigid as his military training dictated.

'What, then, does this tell us about his death?'

'The poison was injected directly into his bloodstream,' my brother replied evenly, stepping to the bedside and bending over the corpse to see for himself. 'As the heart pumped the contaminated blood through his body, the onset of symptoms and subsequent death was far more efficient than the others.'

148

'He was wanted dead quickly, just like Leslie,' said Andrew softly, looking slightly ashen in the face.

I furrowed my brow in concern. He did not look particularly all right. In fact, he seemed to have only worsened.

John nodded in Andrew's direction. 'That's exactly right. But Holmes, if that is the case, then why— Good Heavens, Andrew, are you quite all right?'

Andrew nodded and waved his hand dismissively, but even as he attempted to reassure us, his legs buckled and he slid partway down the wall. I rushed to his side and allowed him to grip my arm for support as Lestrade pulled out the chair from the desk.

Once seated, Andrew seemed to regain a bit of colour in his face, but I still stood behind him with my hand firmly on his shoulder to keep him from standing up.

With intermittent glances at Andrew's pallor, John continued. 'If that is the case, Holmes, then why was he not simply stabbed, as Leslie was?'

'Perhaps they were killed by two different people, with two different ideas,' offered Nicole. 'We do know that at least two people are involved.'

Miss Camberwell has a valid point,' said Holmes, nodding. 'That has yet to be seen. But we do know that someone wanted this man dead urgently, and we may well have the reason why in this very room.'

I sucked in a breath.

The pocket watch Holmes found.

Some sense of urgency inside Edward had used his last moments to fight the involuntary convulsions in his muscles and clutch for the spot under the pillow where it was hidden. He knew that he would not live to tell whatever it was he knew, so he used his final vestiges of strength to point us towards the secrets he had learned.

Holmes pulled out the object, displaying it on his palm. It glinted gold in the gaslight, engraved with the cursive letters *E.J.* It seemed far too small to make such a magnitude of difference upon this case.

'Edward's pocket watch?' asked Nicole.

'Indeed, Miss Camberwell. Let us wind it up and see what it has to tell us.'

Holmes deftly opened the cover with a single snap of his wrist, revealing the hour and minute hands, which stood still at ten minutes past two, their stately forms shrouded in the mystery of whether it had been two o'clock in the morning or afternoon.

He took hold of the knob at the side and began to turn it but stopped almost immediately and looked at the watch face, clearly taken aback. Quickly, he turned and set it on the bed, digging into his pockets.

'Holmes?' John questioned, cocking his head in confusion.

'This is most unexpected,' muttered the detective, pulling a small knife from his coat, turning the watch over to pry up the casing. But he faltered as he poised the blade, and I could see why.

There were already scratch marks along the edge, sharp and deliberate. Someone had already done this exact thing, then replaced the casement.

After a moment of hesitation, Holmes proceeded. For if someone had already taken these same actions, then there truly must lie something of importance beyond the shiny barrier.

'Holmes, what is it?' asked Lestrade, watching the detective's movements with great interest.

'Nothing happened,' Andrew replied as Holmes was too absorbed in the work to answer. 'When he wound up the watch, the hands did not move.'

These words alone seemed to tax him greatly, for after speaking he took several deep gulps of air in immediate succession, quelling the nausea that no doubt threatened to overtake his senses. My hand tightened on his shoulder as I was filled once again with guilt for what I had inadvertently done.

'Halloa,' came the soft exclamation of triumph as Holmes held up his findings. 'The mainspring, the gears, the escapement, *none of it is there!* This is what was hidden inside the compartment where they should be.'

He was holding up a small key for all of us to see.

'For the suitcase,' I murmured, and at my words Holmes' eyes flickered to meet mine.

'Precisely my thoughts. Watson, hand me the suitcase at the foot of the bed, would you?'

My brother nodded and bent down to lift the scuffed bag. His eyes narrowed as he exerted more strength. 'Holmes, what would you suppose is in here? It's far heavier than clothes and a few books should be.'

'How the blazes would you know that he had packed clothes and a few books, Doctor Watson?' asked Lestrade incredulously.

'Inspector, do tell me,' replied John wearily as he handed off the suitcase to Holmes, 'did Edward Jamison look to you like the sort of man who would travel without some reading material?'

Lestrade lowered his gaze as Holmes hefted the suitcase onto the desk and fit the key into the left-hand hole. The clasp made a satisfying *click* as the tumblers lined up, and Holmes let out a pleased huff and did the same on the right side.

John made his way to the other side of the bed to gain a better view as Holmes lifted the lid.

Inside the suitcase, neatly stacked, were several paintings with gilded frames. The top one was of a young girl with a curly-haired spaniel by her side. Judging by the dress she was wearing, the painting was no less than one-hundred years old. As Holmes lifted the first one and set it carefully to the side, he revealed another painting from the same period. A landscape view of a bridge over a pond adorned with lily pads. Holmes continued until five paintings were lined up side by side. He turned to Nicole, who had her hand clamped over her mouth.

'Do you recognize these?'

'Yes, these paintings used to hang on the walls upstairs.'

'They were just recently removed, weren't they?' I asked softly. Holmes looked at me strangely, and I shrugged. 'I noticed the bare patches on the walls when we first arrived. The colouring of the wall was very different, so it was obvious that it had only been recently done.'

'Yes, when my mother died, my father had some portraits commissioned based off several photographs we'd had taken during her lifetime. They were supposed to go where these ones had hung previously. My father received a letter last week that the finished portraits would be sent within a fortnight, so he had these taken down in preparation. I overheard him telling Simon that he would most likely be selling these to an art dealer in London on his next trip, and he'd been storing them in his closet until he got the chance to go down there again. They were part of the inheritance he received when my grandfather died, and he never even knew the subjects of the paintings. But... why did Edward have these in his suitcase?'

'He was protecting the key in his dying moments,' I mused. 'Clearly there's something within these paintings that he wanted us to find.'

Andrew, looking substantially less ashen by this time, took one of the paintings, turning it over. I inhaled sharply at what I saw. The backing of the frame had been torn apart and roughly sewn back together, by someone extremely rushed, or had no experience whatsoever with a needle and thread, or possibly both.

'Holmes, may I borrow your knife?' asked Andrew.

Holmes glanced at the back of the painting and made a small noise of discovery before handing over his pocketknife.

Andrew flicked it open and began cutting through the rude stitches. Once he was close enough, he ripped the last couple open to reveal neat stacks of banknotes, of the fifty- and one-hundred-pound denominations.

'Oh my God,' I breathed.

Andrew ripped out the stitches on the back of the other four paintings as well, removing enough banknotes to easily equal half a million pounds.

'No, no it's impossible.' Nicole's voice was squeaky as she shook her head vigorously from side to side. 'Why on earth would Edward have that much money?'

'I don't think he did,' I said without taking more than a second to think. I wasn't confident that I could do anything to help, however. The situation looked very bad. 'Holmes and I were discussing the apparent disrepair of his suitcase. It seemed strange to me that his suitcase, so worn and frayed at the handles, clasps, and corners from much travel and repeatedly being loaded onto carriages and trains, is so much more scuffed than the rest of his clothes.

'His suit was well-tailored, his shoes shined to perfection. Everything about him spoke of his wealthy background, except his suitcase. From that we can infer that he had enough money to keep himself looking neat for business, but not enough to afford any other small luxuries. This money was not his.'

'No, but a great deal of it should have been,' came a voice from just outside the door.

Chapter 17: Wherever Truth May Lead

We are not afraid to follow truth wherever it may lead, nor to tolerate any error so long as reason is left free to combat it.
— *Thomas Jefferson*

Holmes and Lestrade pulled their guns quickly from their pockets, and Andrew's hand rested on the one he'd stolen from outside the mines. John reached outside the door and roughly pulled in a dirty-faced young man with badly torn sleeves.

'Easy, now! It's not as if I wasn't about to come quietly.'

Andrew reached back and pulled me behind him, making a move to do the same to Nicole, but she wrenched free and took a step towards the man.

'Victor?'

His gaze snapped to her, and sorrow entered his eyes. 'I'm sorry.'

'Andrew, kindly relinquish your seat to this man. I daresay he has a lot to tell us,' Holmes said evenly, keeping his gun pointed straight at Victor.

Andrew nodded and stood up, wobbling slightly. My hand went to his arm again to hold him steady.

'You need not point that weapon at me, Mr Holmes,' Victor said calmly, taking the seat with steady movements. 'I am entirely out of bullets.'

Holmes did not look as if he believed a word of this man's reassurance, and he nodded to John. 'Watson, take his weapon.'

Victor visibly bit his tongue against saying or doing something to antagonise the detective, instead raising his hands slightly as my brother reached into his jacket to pull out his revolver.

'He's right, Holmes, it's empty. The weapon is much too light,' John popped the cylinder open to illustrate, exposing the empty chambers.

'You were the other shooter in the forest, weren't you?' Andrew asked, looking down at Victor with a grimace. I wasn't sure if it was more disgust or nausea from standing upright.

'Well, I must congratulate you on your aim. You managed to keep me dancing on my toes,' Victor replied, looking Andrew up and down appraisingly. 'You must not have noticed I was trying not to hit anyone. I say, you don't look very well.'

'That's… not really connected,' I interjected, giving Andrew enough time to breathe deeply for a few seconds.

'Not *really?*' Victor raised an eyebrow in curiosity.

'All right, enough with the small talk.' Lestrade looked vaguely impatient. 'What in God's name is going on here?'

'Yes, I would quite like an explanation myself,' Holmes said, arms crossed, weapon lowered. 'You are Victor Hughes, are you not?'

Nicole's head shot up. 'How do you know his surname?'

155

'I found his name and address in your brother's chambers. It was not overly difficult.'

'I am,' replied Victor with a solemn nod.

'What were you doing in the woods, Mr Hughes?'

'I was making sure that she did not double back to the mines.' He nodded his head in my direction, and I inhaled sharply.

'And why could you not risk that?'

'So that Leslie's body could be safely dragged away. God rest his soul.' Victor bowed his head and crossed himself.

'Did you not kill Leslie Godwin?'

'I did not kill him, Mr Holmes, but I know that it had to be done, and I despise that very much.'

'Why did it have to be done?'

'He backed away from our deal. He said the risks were too high.'

'The risks of being caught?'

'Yes, sir.'

'Holmes, why do I feel as if you know a good deal more than us?' John asked.

'Come now, Watson, the answer is quite obvious.'

Had my eyes not been largely fixed on Holmes and Victor, I could have sworn that I saw John raise his eyes to the ceiling in a long-suffering prayer.

'You believed that you were being cheated out of the money, didn't you?' The gears in my mind had been working towards the answer for the past several moments.

'The money from the deal with my father?' Nicole asked.

'Yes, and we were,' Victor replied, bitterness in his voice. 'The sums seemed all right at first, but as the amount of lead being mined grew, our share of the profits shrank. I daresay greed got the best of the old man.'

156

'So why did you not just confront him, or report the scandal to the police?' Andrew asked from beside me, his voice growing slightly steadier.

'We should have done such a thing. My God, we should have. But when we met to discuss our best course of action, we foolishly decided that Mr Camberwell would likely refuse, and that if we went to the police, they would rather side with the party with the greater wealth to his name. That night, when we met at the *Black Kettle,* we had intended to confront Simon about the issue, in hopes that he might give us some justice and peace of mind.'

'But instead you killed him,' Nicole spat out bitterly.

'Nicole, I swear to you, we did not kill your brother. We finished our drinks and left the pub. It was our plan to ask him about the money after we left. However, none of us expected to drink as much as we did.

'Instead of confronting Simon about his father cheating us, Edward directly accused him of being behind the whole thing. He threatened him, told him he'd make him pay if he didn't hand over the money that very night. He included some other things, none of which I'd ever dare to repeat. Simon took the threats quite literally, as intoxicated as he was – as we all were. He pulled out his pocketknife and began to brandish it at Edward.

' *"Back off,"* he said. *"Back off or I'll cut your throat."* Edward snatched the knife away from him. Simon lunged to get it back and, frightened, Edward leapt back and slashed at Simon, catching him across the shoulder. Simon clutched at it and staggered back, but it wasn't very serious. He took the knife back and said he didn't know anything about our shares being cut, and after this, he wasn't sure he cared. Then he turned and went back towards the woods and that was the last we saw of him.'

John was shaking his head. 'But someone slipped poison into his drink. If it wasn't you or Edward, who was it? Leslie?'

'It wasn't Leslie, or Patrick. We had specifically planned not to hurt Simon. We only wanted our money. No one was ever supposed to get hurt.'

'So, you didn't kill Mr Camberwell, either?' I asked, feeling quite confused about the whole situation.

Victor's head jerked in my direction. 'Wait, Mr Camberwell's dead too?'

'Mr Hughes, what exactly was Leslie doing when you killed him, and what is Mr Donnelly's – Patrick's – part in all of this?' Holmes asked, his face a blank slate, giving no indication as to the emotions underneath the surface.

'It was the four of us – Leslie, Patrick, Edward, and myself – who were planning this thing. Before Edward sent us the message, we had no idea that Simon was dead. Edward coming here in response to Nicole's letter was the perfect excuse for him to confront Mr Camberwell himself about the money. Hold on, you can't be insinuating that the confrontation went south, and Edward killed him!'

'No one is insinuating anything, Mr Hughes,' Holmes reassured him.

'Edward couldn't have killed him,' I said, shaking my head. 'Mr Camberwell was poisoned, the same as Simon and Edward. If Edward did not kill Simon, then he most certainly would not have killed Mr Camberwell in the same manner.'

'And for that matter,' Andrew added, 'if Simon and Mr Camberwell were killed concerning this, then who killed Edward?'

Holmes held up a hand. 'One matter at a time. Mr Hughes, please continue with your story.'

'When Nicole wrote to Edward that Simon was dead, he immediately wrote the rest of us. He was panicked, thinking he was inadvertently responsible. By the time we received word, he had dropped everything to come here, and we followed, only hoping that he would remember on his own to speak to Mr Camberwell.'

Nicole sighed. 'Victor, by the time Edward arrived, my father was already dead. He died the same day we found Simon's body. Edward arrived as we were burying the both of them in the family plot behind the house.'

Victor shook his head. 'This doesn't make any sense. If Edward didn't resolve the situation with Mr Camberwell, then where did the money come from?'

'*All in due time, Mr Hughes,*' said Holmes slowly and firmly. 'What was Mr Godwin doing in the mines? Why did he need to be killed?'

'If Edward couldn't get the money back, he was just going to take what was rightfully ours, and we would divide it between ourselves. Leslie backed out. He said the risks of being caught were too much. If we were caught and turned in, not only would we be jailed, but we'd get nothing. I suppose with Mr Camberwell dead, that's the case anyway.

'Edward was supposed to meet us in the mines to divide the money. Leslie, Patrick and I were waiting there for him. While we were waiting, Leslie told us that he couldn't handle it. He said that if we went through with it, he would turn us in, hoping they would give him a deal. Patrick pulled out his knife and stabbed him.

'I wanted no part of it, not now that there was murder involved. I tried to leave through the closest entrance, but I heard voices coming through the trees. That would be you and your friends, Nicole. I knew that I couldn't leave without crossing your path, so I turned around and went to warn Patrick that he needed to stash Leslie's body and run. We waited until you were at the main entrance, then I slipped out through the other side – where you three must have exited. Patrick was to cause a distraction and run.'

159

'A distraction?' Andrew interjected. '*A distraction?* He set off dynamite and blocked the entrance!'

Victor looked vaguely uncomfortable. 'Yes, well... I had no part in that decision. After he escaped, we met outside, on the path to the town. He said that I had made the decision to be involved and I couldn't back out, or he would kill me too. We waited until you came out and headed back towards the house, and then we went in to retrieve the body. We didn't expect you to come back, and not with help. I covered the outside – I was the one who followed you out into the woods – while Patrick stood ground against the others inside. I assume that would be you three?' He looked up at Holmes, John, and Lestrade, who looked back at him with cold expressions.

'Where is Mr Donnelly?' Lestrade asked, his face hard but his eyes tired.

'I don't know where Patrick is. I can only assume that he retreated with the body.'

'Mr Hughes, why are you telling us all this?' John asked. 'Why not run instead of coming here to confess?'

'Edward never showed up with the money. I'm no fool. I knew that Patrick would somehow be caught for Leslie's murder, and I knew that as the only other remaining member of our group, I would be suspected alongside him. It was obvious that Edward had either given up and turned us all in, that he'd made off with the money on his own, or that something had happened to him. I knew I wasn't getting any profit from any of those possibilities, so I decided it was best to come clean. My God, I didn't expect Edward to be dead as well. What in God's name happened?'

'He was poisoned,' answered Lestrade. 'The same as Mr Camberwell and his son. Speaking of which, Holmes, how in God's name do you presume to explain that?'

Holmes' eyes glinted, and he held up a finger. 'I think it obvious that Mr Jamison was planning to run with the money. It

160

was concealed in his suitcase, and not just in stacks – as it would have been if he had been planning to meet his confederates at all – but inside the backs of paintings, for an extra layer of protection. If someone happened to see the contents of his suitcase, he could simply pose as an art dealer heading for London or another metropolis instead of having to explain away thousands of pounds in Bank of England notes.'

John groaned. 'Holmes, this is all very well and good, but why was he killed? Why were any of them killed?'

'Patience is a virtue, Watson! It is quite plain if you take a closer look at these notes. Do you see the loops on the G?' He held up one of the stacks for our inspection. 'Last year, the Bank made a series of changes, including changing the structure of the lettering completely. Only, these notes are dated *this year.*'

'They're counterfeit,' Andrew breathed.

'Precisely! Whoever printed these notes inked in a current date to explain the fresh texture and make it seem as if they hadn't been in circulation for long, only they printed it using old plates.'

'But couldn't Mr Camberwell have already had the notes, not knowing they were counterfeit?' Lestrade furrowed his brow.

Nicole shook her head. 'No, my father always took the receipts from his profits to the bank two towns over and had them print the money. If this was money he was withholding from the others, it would have come directly from there.'

Holmes nodded, the corners of his mouth twitching upwards. 'The scratches which were already on the back of the watch have two distinct groove patterns. One is obviously from when Mr Jamison first removed the casement to conceal the key to the suitcase. But the other, from whence did it come? Mr Jamison attempted to shield this key until his dying breath. It stands to reason that he knew someone was after the money, which at this stage could not have been counterfeit.'

'So, someone pried off the cover on the watch to remove the key after his death,' Victor concluded. 'Then they took out the money and replaced it with counterfeit. But why? Why go to all that trouble, and why kill for the money when it could have simply been stolen in the first place?'

'To make it seem like all of it was part of the same scheme,' I said automatically. 'That way the culprit could escape with the money while we wasted time trying to pin it on Simon's remaining friends.'

'Which means they could very well be long gone by now,' Lestrade growled, murmuring an expletive and kicking at the bedpost in frustration.

Holmes looked distant, but he shook it off and held up a hand. 'We still have an arrest to make, for the murder of Leslie Godwin. Mr Hughes, do you have *any* idea where Patrick Donnelly might be?'

Victor averted his eyes for a moment, tapping his foot as he thought. 'Our plan was to take the body back to the mine and throw it into the unused shaft. The smell of the ores would mask the decay, and they'd never find it as long as that shaft remained abandoned. After that we would gather our things from our room at the inn in town and catch the next train. We didn't have time to worry about finding Edward and the money. Not after Leslie. If he's anywhere, it'll be the inn.'

It took a while to find the coachman and persuade him to drive our company into town. But finally, we arrived in front of the Rosedale Inn, a shabby little wooden structure that looked as if it had been erected solely for the purpose of having an inn, rather than being intended for frequent use. I doubted that this dusty, foul-smelling mining town was a popular holiday destination.

'Good evening, Mrs Doonesbury,' said Victor loudly to the old woman who was snoozing in a threadbare armchair inside. Her face was heavily darkened and wrinkled with age, so riddled with warts that at first glance she might appear to be a gnarled tree.

She started slightly at his voice and awoke. Sighting Victor, her eyes lit up and she opened her mouth in a crooked, rotting smile.

'Might I have the spare key to our room?' the man asked in the same loud, precise voice. 'I seem to have misplaced mine, and Mr Donnelly might not be there.'

Mrs Doonesbury nodded and pulled herself to her feet, holding up a finger as she shuffled off into another room. She returned a moment later bearing a dusty key with the number 3 messily etched into it.

'Thank you, Mrs Doonesbury,' said Victor, taking the key and giving her a slight bow. He then turned to us. 'All right, let's see if he's here. You'll all need to stay behind me as I open the door. I fear he'll make for the window.'

Holmes nodded, and Lestrade hesitated a moment, but eventually gave in, resting his hand on his revolver as we ascended the narrow, rickety staircase in single file.

Victor stopped in front of the third door and tried the doorknob. It didn't budge, and he cursed under his breath, raising his fist to rap sharply.

'Patrick? It's Victor. Are you in there?'

No answer came and Victor unlocked the door slowly.

'My God!' he exclaimed upon entering the room, and Holmes, John, and Lestrade followed, hands poised to draw their weapons, the rest of us close behind.

A man I could only assume to be Patrick lay on the floor, brow beaded with sweat and eyes glazed over in fever, his arms and legs twitching sporadically. His lips and fingers were tinged blue. A bottle of whiskey lay spilt on the table in the corner. Blood was crusted on his shoulder.

As John knelt beside him, I needed no help in deciphering the scene before us. Patrick had been the one shot in the mines. He disposed of the body and returned here to tend to his wound as best he could. He drank the bottle of whiskey to dull the pain, but it must have been poisoned, and it took effect before he could do anything.

'Watson, is there anything you can do for him?' Holmes asked urgently, bending down beside my brother to assess the damage.

John looked into the detective's eyes desperately. 'No, nothing. He's already deep in the throes of the toxin. There's not enough time to search for an antidote. He's as good as gone.'

Indeed, almost as he spoke, Patrick Donnelly's rapid breathing grew slower and shallower, almost rasping, and finally stopped altogether. His limbs stopped twitching and his head fell limply to the side, bleeding slightly from the mouth.

Nicole's hands flew to cover her mouth. She buried her face in my shoulder to shield herself from the sight. Andrew's hand grasped mine, and with my free arm I reached to soothe her, although I was numb with horror.

John's head drooped visibly as he closed Patrick's eyes and placed his limp hands over his chest.

Holmes straightened up and ran a hand over his face. I knew that he was liable to blame himself for a death he could have prevented had he only acted sooner. We all were. To strive for perfection was a human instinct, and not one that Sherlock Holmes took lightly.

He paced around the room in brooding silence for a moment, before turning to Victor.

'Mr Hughes, whoever is responsible for this is tying up their loose ends. You are the only piece remaining. We will be returning to London first thing in the morning. Inspector Lestrade will place you under arrest for conspiracy to commit theft and murder. You will return to London with us, where the inspector will file a warrant for your official custody until this is sorted out. You will not leave our sight, is this understood?'

Victor nodded, visibly shaken. 'Who could be doing this?'

'I cannot say at this juncture,' replied Holmes, 'but I promise we will do everything in our power to follow where truth may lead.'

By this time, my adrenaline was beginning to wear off, and I could tell that Nicole's was too. John was not oblivious to this fact, and he urged Andrew to escort us back to the Abbey to get some rest before the morning's trip.

The ride back to the house was very quiet. The only sound was the shuffling of our feet on the floor of the coach, coated with rust-red dust from the mines. When we arrived, Andrew softly thanked the coachman and ushered Nicole and I up the steps.

Halfway up, when Nicole was a long way ahead of us, I stopped and grabbed Andrew's arm.

'Andrew, the loose ends, the deaths. Something feels dreadfully familiar about this. You don't think—'

Andrew looked into my eyes and sighed deeply. 'Emily, this is the path of any killer who wants to leave himself undetected, not just Moriarty. If you doubt this, I'm sure Holmes can tell you, in all his years of working cases, not everything is connected to some darker conspiracy. Now come on, let's all go get some rest.'

He took my hand and led me up the remainder of the steps, and I sighed. Perhaps he was right. It was completely illogical that Moriarty could be behind this as well. He had no plausible connections to it, and tying up loose ends was not a factor unique to his dealings.

Yet, as Andrew held open the large door for me, and I took another look back at the dark trees in the distance, I could not help but picture more sinister forces, working underground to capture what otherwise might not have been theirs.

A chill crept down my spine as Andrew placed a hand on my shoulder, and I turned and entered the house.

Epilogue: What of the Night?

Watchman, what of the night?
— Isaiah 21:11

The next morning, the sun rose over the trees outside, letting solitary rays of light filter across the lawn. As the first beam drew a line across the floor, our company stood in the entryway of Rosedale Abbey, watching as the coachman carried our luggage out to the waiting carriage.

Victor's hands were cuffed together in front of him, and Lestrade stood to the side, talking to Andrew quietly.

I understood the Inspector's motivations for the cuffs on Victor, although I had a feeling that the man knew what a foolish idea it would be to run from the only men who were currently offering him protection from whomever might be after him.

Moriarty, whispered a voice in my head. *Moriarty is after him.*

168

No. Absolutely not. I took a deep breath and cleansed my thoughts. It wasn't him. There was no evidence, no reason.

I turned to Nicole. 'Will you be all right? Is there anyone besides the staff here who could come stay with you?'

'Actually, yes.' She pulled a pristinely addressed envelope from her pocket. 'Will you take this to London and mail it for me? I have an older sister, Lucy. I… hadn't had time to mention it. She's studying abroad in America. This is a letter alerting her of the events and requesting her presence back at home.'

She pressed the envelope into my hand, her eyes meeting mine in an expression of trust. I placed my hand on top of hers and gave a small smile.

'I will. Stay safe, please.'

Nicole gave me a quick embrace, as we observed that the others were deliberately moving towards the doors.

'I shall. Goodbye, Emily.'

I took another look at her and smiled as we pulled apart. Then, I slipped my hand into Andrew's and walked away.

On the train back to London, we separated into two compartments. Lestrade, Victor and John took one, while Holmes, Andrew and I took another.

It wasn't as if we couldn't have all had our own compartments. We were the only ones on the train. I doubted it even would have run had we not showed up at the station. But Victor couldn't be alone, and no one else wanted to be, quite understandably.

After a long while of sitting in silence, Andrew made a small grunting noise and stood, looking down at me. 'I'm going to step out and stretch my legs. Would you like to come?'

I looked up, a little startled by the sudden words.

'All right,' I replied, taking his hand.

As I followed him out of the compartment, adjusting to the rumble of the wheels on the track beneath me, I could sense Holmes' eyes on me, and I knew exactly what they were saying.

Are you going to tell him?

I straightened my shoulders and ignored it.

There were sets of windows across the corridor, and we wandered down the hall, silent, but grateful for the ability to stretch our cramped legs.

We stopped at one of the windows, looking out at the barren landscape speeding by, watching it grow steadily greener as we progressed south.

After a few moments, Andrew spoke. 'Did you see me talking to Lestrade before we left?'

I broke my gaze out the window and looked up at him. 'As a matter of fact, I did. What was it about?'

He sighed. 'He received word that my father stepped down as Commissioner.'

I inhaled sharply. 'What? Why? Did something happen?'

Andrew gave me a small smile. 'Nothing of scandalous or ruining proportions, if that's what you're thinking. He was offered a better position. As an advisor to the Home Secretary.'

'That's fantastic,' I replied, breathless. 'But what's going to happen to you? You won't still be able to spend your days at the Yard, am I right?'

'Well, I've been considering it for some time,' he said after a moment, taking a cleansing breath. 'I'm going to pursue a career as an officer. It may not play out right away, but that's all right. I just know it's what I want. I've already come close enough.'

'How long before a new Commissioner is appointed?'

'According to Lestrade, one is already being considered. He has only to accept the offer.'

'I'm very happy for you. Both of you.' I placed my hand on top of his.

As I shifted, I felt a weight in my pocket and sucked in a breath in confusion. What on earth could that be?

'I'm going to sit back down,' said Andrew after a beat of silence.

'You go on,' I told him softly. 'I'll be there in a moment.'

He nodded and set off back down the corridor.

Once he was out of sight, I dug into my pocket and pulled out the object. It was the ivory-handled knife I'd found in the forest the night before. I turned it over with bated breath and peered at the initials.

S.M.

What on Earth could they stand for? I knew of no one with those initials, certainly none who had been involved with this case.

I leaned against the wall, willing myself to think of any connection.

When nothing came, I returned to our compartment. I sat back in my seat and closed my eyes, focusing on the rhythmic jostle of the railcar, and eventually I drifted off to sleep.

When I awoke with a start, the scenery outside the window was growing more urban by the minute. It was clear that we were growing close to the city limits of London.

I tucked an errant strand of hair behind my ear, struggling to remember the details of my dream.

Or was it completely a dream?

It had taken place when I had been kidnapped by Moriarty, the evening he had requested my presence for dinner. As I entered the room, my escort by my side, Moriarty and another man were whispering urgently to each other. Before they looked up, I could make out a name. Sebastian Moran.

S.M.

As the memory sucked away my breath, Holmes cleared his throat. 'Good, you're awake.'

I looked around. Andrew was gone again. A glance through the small window of our compartment confirmed that he was in the corridor, conversing with Lestrade. John must be with Victor.

'What is it?' I asked, inhaling deliberately.

Holmes leaned forward, his eyes betraying with a flick towards the door that he did not want to be overheard. 'Why do you think that part of the mine was abandoned, Emily?'

I furrowed my brow. '...Because the supply of lead was exhausted?'

'If they ran out of lead, they would tunnel deeper until they found more. Something made them stop that direction and move all their resources immediately to the other side instead of forging a connecting passage.'

I thought of all the debris we had seen at the entrance. 'They found something they shouldn't have.'

'Exactly. And we trod right on top of it. It's on our shoes, and Andrew's vest.'

'Dried blood is on Andrew's vest.'

'Those streaks on the wall weren't blood, Emily. Not all of them, anyway. *Look at our shoes.*'

My gaze dropped to the floor. Our shoes were still caked around the edges with reddish-brown dirt. 'Clay? What's so bad about that?'

'That's not clay, Emily. I'll test a sample once we return to Baker Street, but I'm positive of its identity. It's cinnabar. Hepatic cinnabar, to be exact.'

'Cinnabar? You mean the rock they powdered to colour ancient stoneware? Isn't it highly toxic?'

'Indeed. It's composed of mercury sulphide, and its dangers have been known since ancient Roman times. Which is precisely why the mine shaft would have been abandoned as soon as they hit upon a vein of it.'

'Then doesn't that solve the problem?'

'Unless they didn't abandon the area soon enough. Hepatic cinnabar is impure, but no less potent. It is more brown than scarlet and is softer, mixed with other earthy matter. When it was uncovered, someone likely dismissed it as clay – much like you did.'

'Then what?'

'Last night, when Watson returned before me, I stayed in town to ask around. A month ago, three miners died. Each had complained of severe chest pains and shortness of breath – common symptoms for miners – for a few days before the symptoms escalated. One man contracted the fastest acting case of pneumonia I've ever heard of. He was short of breath in the morning, began coughing up blood in the afternoon, and was dead by dinner. The second man woke in the night, screaming about a giant monster stealing his breath, and would let no one near him until he collapsed into a seizure, became unresponsive, and died. The third man hadn't slept in days, ranting about being stalked by red men from the hills. In his hysteria, he had shot himself in the head. All three passed away within five days of each other.'

'Mercury poisoning.'

Holmes nodded. 'Once it became obvious, I'm sure Mr Camberwell and the mine overseers cleared everyone out in the middle of the day. But suppose someone else knew, and threatened to tell the Press?'

'They'd have to be kept quiet. Blackmailed.'

'Or murdered.'

I averted my gaze, thinking. Mr Camberwell wouldn't have told; he was the one who needed it to stay quiet. Simon, as well, had too much to lose. Leslie was killed by Patrick because he refused to take the money. That left Edward or Patrick.

'But why?' I asked. 'If they were killed to keep them quiet, then whomever killed them wanted the mines to stay open, not closed. Besides, what happens to the mines with the owner and all presumptive heirs dead?'

'They go up for sale,' Holmes replied. 'If the mines close because of deaths linked to mercury sulphide, then whomever had their eye on them loses out on a sizable fortune.'

Someone wanted those mines very badly, and took the opportunity to make off with the money Mr Camberwell had been embezzling as well. I was about to ask Holmes who he thought could be behind it when the compartment door opened, and he leaned back, lips closed tightly.

Andrew was back, bringing the conversation to a close.

The next day, back at Baker Street, I was reading an old monograph of Holmes's – *A Study of Deciduous Trees in Britain* – as John sat at his desk, scribbling away at a stack of papers.

Holmes entered, returning from Mrs Hudson's call that the post was waiting downstairs, and peered over John's shoulder. 'What have we here, Watson?'

'It's nothing,' John assured him, looking rather flustered.

'Nonsense! What's this?' Holmes picked up a sheet of paper to the side of the tall stack. ' *"A Study in Scarlet, Being a*

Reprint from the Reminiscences of John H. Watson, M.D., Late of the Army Medical Department." A memoir of the Jefferson Hope case! How fantastically lurid, Watson.'

He slapped the paper back down on the desk and flopped melodramatically into his armchair to open the mail.

I set aside the monograph and took a sip of tea, stretching on the sofa and staring into the crackling embers of the fireplace. I was grateful for the emanating warmth that protected us from the frigid winds outside.

John was once again deeply engrossed in his writing by the time Holmes reached a short missive that made him stop and murmur, 'By God!'

'What is it?' I asked, setting down my teacup.

'It's a note from Lestrade. Victor Hughes was found dead in his cell this morning. It appears that he hanged himself.'

My eyes widened, startled. 'Do you believe that report?'

He set the letter aside, leaning forward and steepling his fingers gravely. 'Not even a little.'

Later that afternoon, I donned my cloak and set off to postmark the letter Nicole had asked me to send to her sister in America. As I was leaving the post office on Wigmore Street, a stack of newspapers on the ground caught my attention. It had undoubtedly been abandoned by some newsboy who had found something better to do with his time.

I bent down to pick one up, staring at the headline which had sparked my interest:

Highly Acclaimed Professor Purchases Yorkshire Mine.

No. Surely not. I skimmed the article, hoping against all reason.

...a celebrity in the scientific community, Professor James Moriarty, formerly of the University of St Andrews, Scotland, announced last night his purchase of a mine in North Yorkshire, previously owned by the late Oliver Camberwell.

Having recently come into a great sum of money, Professor Moriarty made a wise and deliberate move to purchase the rights and funding to a mine which would otherwise have been condemned by the government in a matter of days, surely a welcome prospect to the surrounding community of Rosedale Abbey and the dozens of people who have made working the mine their choice of labour.

Breathless, I dropped the paper back on the ground and walked briskly away, aware of an all-too-familiar man with a dark and weathered face watching me from a short distance.

I caught his reflection in the post office window. It was the same man whom I had seen through the trees the day of the funeral at the Camberwell's, and suddenly I remembered where I had seen him before.

He had been the one hiding in Nicole's room the night I had been knocked unconscious. The blurry face from my dream on the train shifted into focus and I wanted nothing more than to get as far away from him as I could as it dawned on me with sickening clarity who he was.

The name *Sebastian Moran* fit his countenance like a glove.

I repressed a shudder as I picked up my pace, hoping desperately that he would not follow me.

Perhaps Andrew was wrong after all. It is the suggestion of many philosophers that there is a deeper, hidden meaning behind everything that happens in our lives. Some unseen force that constantly shadows us, manipulating our every move.

Whether this force's name was Fate or Moriarty remained to be seen.